"You won't regret staying."

Mae Parker's words echoed in Claire's mind as she waited while her patient napped. The words had been meant as reassurance—a promise, even. But Claire had learned long ago not to put faith in promises. All too often they were forgotten, or never meant in the first place. Life was easier when taken one minute, one hour at a time.

She wished Mae Parker well, as she did all her patients. But the woman would be no different from the other patients Claire had cared for over the years. When her services were no longer needed she'd leave the Parker Ranch in the same state as she'd arrived—with her emotions intact.

Because that was a lesson she'd also learned a long time ago. *She* was the only person she could rely on.

ABOUT THE AUTHOR

Although Ginger Chambers currently resides outside Texas, from accent to attitude she's still very much a product of the Lone Star State—and proud of it! "Writing a book set in Texas is almost as good as being there," Ginger says. "The Parkers of West Texas have become family. I love each and every one of them." But all good things must come to an end—this will be the final book in THE WEST TEXANS series she's enjoyed. Here's hoping you enjoy reading about the Parkers as much as she's enjoyed creating them.

You can visit Ginger at the Web site www.superauthors.com or contact her at gingerchambers@superauthors.com.

A message from Ginger Chambers: May is national Get Caught Reading month. I can think of few things more rewarding and more fun than stepping into a new world with characters who make you laugh or make you cry or keep you on the edge of your seat wondering what's going to happen next. Come along for the ride! Read a book!

Books by Ginger Chambers

HARLEQUIN SUPERROMANCE
680—A MATCH MADE IN TEXAS
730—WEST TEXAS WEDDINGS
778—TEXAS LAWMAN
820—TWILIGHT, TEXAS
862—BORN IN TEXAS
907—HIDDEN IN TEXAS

Texas Forever
Ginger Chambers

HARLEQUIN®

TORONTO • NEW YORK • LONDON
AMSTERDAM • PARIS • SYDNEY • HAMBURG
STOCKHOLM • ATHENS • TOKYO • MILAN • MADRID
PRAGUE • WARSAW • BUDAPEST • AUCKLAND

ISBN 0-373-70989-7

TEXAS FOREVER

Copyright © 2001 by Ginger Chambers.

This edition published by arrangement with Harlequin Books S.A.

Visit us at www.eHarlequin.com

Printed in U.S.A.

Texas Forever

CHAPTER ONE

"I DON'T NEED A baby-sitter," Mae Parker declared imperiously from the wingback chair where she sat across from Claire Hannaford. "In fact, if every time I turn around you're there, I'm not gonna like it. What I need is for you to act as my backup. I'll tell you where I'm goin' and how long I plan to be there, and if I don't show up when I'm supposed to, you come lookin' for me. But I don't want you with me every minute. I can take perfectly good care of myself. Except—" her shoulders twitched "—for when I'm havin' one of my spells."

Claire shifted slightly on the couch. She had not expected such a vigorous client. The head of the home health care agency where she was registered had informed her with gushing excess of the Parker family's importance in far West Texas and of the matriarch's—Mae Parker's—long-time political influence across the state, but she'd told her very little of the woman's actual physical condition. The usual Q and A collected about a client's health history had been overlooked in the haste to accommodate Mae Parker.

"I was told when you called the agency, you said you'd fallen in the bathtub," Claire replied evenly. "Were you injured?"

"My pride was."

"Nothing else?"

"I bruised my hip and an elbow."

"You were lucky. They could've been broken."

"I'm aware of that."

Mae Parker seemed remarkable for her years. Her mind was clear, her posture erect, her tone commanding. Even at ninety-one, the force of her personality radiated throughout the room.

"Does your doctor know about these...spells?" Claire asked.

"He knows. He just looks at me and shakes his head."

Claire decided to be direct. She didn't want to be a baby-sitter any more than Mae Parker wanted one. Too many people were in real need of help for her to waste her time with someone who wasn't.

"Considering what you've said, Miss Parker, wouldn't it be better to ask a family member to act as your backup? Why hire me—a nurse?"

"Because I *want* a nurse."

Claire tried another tack. "Tell me about these spells."

"I get a little light-headed on occasion."

"Enough that you fall?"

"The tub was slippery."

"What does your family think about you hiring a nurse?" Along with the flow of information about the family's status, Claire had also been told they were a tightly knit group.

The woman's shoulders twitched again, but she gave no reply.

"They *are* concerned, aren't they?" Claire pressed.

"Of course they're concerned! They're concerned too darned much! Been in a tizzy ever since I fell. Been after me to—"

Claire frowned at the terminated sentence. "I don't—" she began.

She'd been going to say "understand," but the matriarch broke in with a prescient, "You don't *have* to understand. You just have to be willin' to help!"

Everything about Mae Parker gave witness to the fact that she was a proud woman—a strong woman, one accustomed to being in charge. For her to admit that her life needed monitoring couldn't have been easy.

The woman's hawklike eyes watched Claire as

she considered what she would do. She thought for a moment to refuse. But the agency had sent her here to do a job and she would do it. "I'm willing," she said.

A satisfied smile tugged at the older woman's thin lips. "Then I'll have Axel bring in your luggage."

"I have a trunk."

"A trunk," Mae Parker repeated.

"A wardrobe trunk, fitted to the top of my car."

"Good thing Axel's a big man. You'll be usin' the parlor off my bedroom while you're here. We've moved a few things...put in a single bed. Will that be satisfactory?"

"Certainly," Claire agreed.

The woman cocked her head and examined her more closely. "There's somethin' different about you. You're very...calm."

"My charges often find that soothing."

"I'm not complainin', mind you. It's probably a good thing, what with the family likely to have another tizzy when they hear about you. Maybe you'll be able to *soothe* them."

"My being here will upset them?" Claire asked.

"Oh, they'll get used to it," Mae Parker said, then stood up with the aid of a shiny black cane. "Now, I'm sorry to put this on you before you've barely had a chance to catch your breath, but news travels fast in these parts, and I want at least some of 'em to hear what's goin' on direct from me. I'll deal with the others later.''

Claire rose slowly as her new employer started for the door. She was tired. The drive from Midland to the ranch had been longer and more difficult than she'd expected. Especially the last leg, where few markers guided the way. The Parker Ranch was in the middle of nowhere. More than once she'd almost despaired of completing her journey the same day.

Mae Parker paused, and mistaking Claire's weariness for hesitancy, explained, ''I've sent word for a few of 'em to come over so I can introduce you. They might make some noise, but no one'll bite.''

Together, the two women walked down the hall. Normally Claire settled into a job with little fanfare. If her charge had a family—a big *if* in most cases—there were rarely more than one or two members. And they were greatly relieved to have someone to help.

They passed through the Spanish-style entryway and entered a large living room where a small group of people waited.

All eyes locked on Claire.

Mae Parker wasted no time. ''Everyone, this is Claire Hannaford...my new nurse. Claire—'' she pointed from one person to another ''—this is

Rafe, my great-nephew and the manager of the ranch. Next to him is LeRoy, another great-nephew. Next to LeRoy is Harriet, his wife, and next to her on the couch is Rafe's wife, Shannon. They all live in the ranch compound, like me.''

Claire's gaze moved, quietly curious, over each of the four people. Rafe was long and lean and in his early to mid-forties. He had the same strikingly chiseled features as Mae, mostly dark hair and dark eyes. LeRoy was shorter and stockier than his cousin, a year or so younger and with the same Parker ''look.'' Harriet was a sturdy brunette; Shannon a slim, blue-eyed blonde. All of them stared back at her as if thunderstruck.

''It's very nice to meet you,'' Claire said into the lengthening silence.

''*A nurse!*'' Rafe burst out, jerking forward in his chair.

Mae bristled. ''You heard what I said. I don't know why you're all so surprised! You've been after me for the last couple of weeks to *do* something. And now that I have, you act like the next thing you'll be doin' is kickin' dirt in on my grave!''

The outrageous assertion brought instant protests.

''Aunt Mae!''

''We're not—''

"You're not—"

Mae lifted a quelling hand. "I've made up my mind, and that's that!"

"But, Aunt Mae," Harriet appealed. "You know our Gwen would be happy to spend nights over here. And Shannon and I can take turns keepin' an eye out in the day. Jodie'll be glad to take her turn, too. So will Christine and Delores. You don't have to look outside the family. We *want* to help you...in any way we can."

"Harriet's right, Mae," Shannon agreed. "If you'd just let us, we'd—"

Mae Parker would have none of it. "Most of you have your hands full with babies and such, and those that don't—" she moved quickly to foil another protest by Harriet "—have other things to worry about. No, this is the way I want things done." She glanced toward Claire. "If you keep makin' a fuss, you're gonna make Claire think she's not welcome."

Harriet, too, sent Claire a quick glance. "We didn't mean it that way. It's just—"

"Why didn't you talk to us about what you were thinkin'?" Rafe demanded. "Why keep us in the dark, then spring it on us like this?"

"Because I didn't want any of you tryin' to talk me out of it!"

"We wouldn't have done that!"

Mae glared at him. "Yes, you would. You're tryin' it now!"

Rafe's smoldering dark gaze flicked to Claire, as if he resented having to discuss private family matters in front of a stranger. "I'm not trying anything, Aunt Mae." He ground the words out tightly.

"Good," Mae said, then to change the subject, she looked around the room and demanded, "Where's Tanner? He's supposed to be here, too. LeRoy, go see if you can find him. Marie's probably in the kitchen this minute, tappin' her foot, waitin' to serve the coffee I asked for." The implacable gaze returned to Claire. "Claire, if you're hungry, she can rustle you up whatever you want in two shakes. Just say the word."

Before LeRoy could gain his feet, a man in his mid-thirties stepped into the room. Instead of the western gear the other men had on—serviceable jeans, boots and long-sleeved cotton shirts—he wore a pair of trim-fitting khaki slacks and a rust-colored rough-silk shirt.

Claire noticed right away that he didn't have the Parker "look." He was equally nice looking, but his features were more even, more relaxed. And his brown hair, curling onto the nape of his neck, was casually cut.

"Ah! Tanner! There you are!" Mae exclaimed.

"Now we can go for our coffee. Claire, you sit by me. Tanner, you, too."

They shifted into the adjoining dining room, where the matriarch took primary position at the head of a long highly polished table already set for refreshments. Claire and the man named Tanner seated themselves where directed, while the others took their accustomed places.

Upon their arrival, a plump middle-aged woman with short gray hair bustled in from the kitchen. She carried a silver coffeepot and moved around the table to fill each cup. Her blunt features had been tight all along, but when she served Claire, they grew even tighter.

"Thank you, Marie," Mae said, and the woman bustled off again.

Claire was highly aware that she continued to be the object of everyone's attention. She tried to ignore the curious, sometimes hostile looks, but found it difficult. Finally, Mae Parker shifted the spotlight away from her.

"Tanner," the matriarch barked. "Marie tells me you've only brought one suitcase."

"That's right, only one," he confirmed. He had a nice voice, slightly husky, and an attractive smile.

"Won't you need more than that?" Mae demanded. "What kind of clothes did you bring?

Those you're wearin' now sure aren't good for ridin' a horse.''

"I didn't expect to ride a horse."

The woman's dark eyes moved over her family, causing them to tense, before she again addressed the man. "Just because you're not gettin' to do what you came for…it doesn't mean you can't enjoy yourself. You and your brother and sisters have always been welcome guests on the ranch.''

"I'd rather work for my keep," Tanner said easily.

"Then Rafe can find somethin' *else* for you to do. You can, can't you, Rafe?''

"It'd be a waste of Tanner's time to have him work cattle," Rafe growled from the foot of the table.

"It's better than havin' him work our books!'' Mae shot back. "There's nothing wrong with the way we keep our records. If it's been good enough for the past hundred and more years, it should be good enough today.'' She turned back to Tanner, her fierceness deliberately tamed. "A young man like you shouldn't spend so much time indoors. You need fresh air, sunshine, exercise. You can't get that sittin' in an office starin' at one a' them computers.''

Claire had the strong sense of a giant spider

weaving her web. Or a chess master planning her moves.

"Tanner's done pretty good for himself by doin' just that, Aunt Mae," LeRoy reminded her from his seat next to Claire.

"I never said he hasn't been successful!"

"A computer saved the day back when Shannon put together the family history," Harriet said. "You wouldn't have had 'em to give away that Christmas if you hadn't bought a computer for her to use to finish on time. Remember?"

"I know the darn things have their uses," Mae retorted. "I just don't want one messin' with our ranch records. They're too important!"

"The family history wasn't important?" Shannon asked with feigned innocence.

Mae pointedly returned her attention to Tanner. "As I was sayin'…fresh air and sunshine, that's what you need. And we have both a' those things in abundance. Rafe, have Morgan take Tanner out to Big Spur early this next week. Introduce him to Quint and Katlin. He'll enjoy meetin' 'em, and it'll be a nice ride."

"Tryin' to get him out of the way for a whole day, Aunt Mae?" Rafe challenged. "Takes all day to get to Big Spur and back on a horse," he explained to Tanner.

Mae shifted stiffly. "They can go by pickup for all I care," she claimed.

"Still takes a good bite out of a day," Rafe said.

"I'm just bein' hospitable!"

Claire began to question the wisdom of her decision to stay. It was obvious Mae Parker was playing some kind of power game with her family concerning the ranch records. Was she also using the fact that Claire was a nurse as some kind of leverage to gain her way?

The matriarch noticed her discomfort. "And here we are, bein' inhospitable to our other guest. Claire, I apologize, for myself and my family."

The apology was uttered so smoothly that it underscored Claire's growing misgivings. She refused to be a pawn in anyone's game.

Something bumped her foot. Another foot! Startled, she looked up...into a pair of amused brown eyes. Tanner winked before directing her attention to the head of the table with a brief tip of his head.

Color crept into Claire's cheeks when she realized she'd yet to reply to Mae Parker's apology, and that everyone was looking at her again.

Instead of forcing a reply, though, the matriarch commanded, "Tell us a little something about yourself, Claire."

Claire evaded a direct answer. "There's not much to say."

"You didn't just hatch from an egg! Where were you born...raised? Do you have a large family?"

Leaning forward, Claire said quietly, "Miss Parker, we need to talk."

"Yes, we do. My family and I want to get to know you better."

"Mae," Shannon spoke up, "possibly it would be better to wait. If Claire's uncomfortable—"

The matriarch slapped a hand on the table. "Then we know who to blame, don't we? I told y'all all that arguin' would scare her away!"

Scowling fiercely, Mae was about to say something more when an odd expression crossed her features. She made a soft hissing sound...then slumped back in her chair.

The other Parker women cried out in alarm and rushed to the matriarch's side.

"Don't—don't...fuss." Mae waved them off weakly.

Claire stood up and reached calmly for her charge's wrist. The pulse was thready and weak. "Maybe you should lie down," she suggested. "Have a little rest."

Mae groped for the side of her chair. "My cane," she said, not sounding at all like the woman-in-charge a few minutes ago.

"Here it is," Shannon murmured, and held the cane out to her.

Claire helped the woman to her feet, then bracing the aged body against her own, started for the door.

No one moved at first, still stunned by what had occurred. Finally, Rafe scraped back his chair.

"I can carry her," he offered gruffly.

"Like I said, boy," his great-aunt snapped, "I'm not ready for my grave *yet*."

Harriet, who'd lost most of her natural ruddy color, grasped the back of the chair in front of her and moaned.

Mae tsked in irritation, but Claire doubted the others heard.

Once they moved out of sight of the family, the woman's steps grew more labored. But the greater effort didn't stop her from challenging Claire between breaths as they passed into the entryway. "You were about to change your mind, weren't you? Because you thought I was wastin' your time."

"Where's your bedroom?" Claire asked.

"Next door down from my office."

Claire opened the door onto two nicely appointed rooms. The first was a small and cozy parlor; the second, a much larger bed chamber. Walnut wainscoting ringed the walls, in concert with finely striped paper that echoed the two rooms' decorative accents of cream, coral, green and teal. The only off notes were in the parlor, where a single bed stood in place of a sofa, a chest of drawers was pressed against one wall, and photos and keepsakes had been crowded onto bookshelves. All altered to make room for her.

After settling her charge into a chair in the bedroom, Claire turned down the satin comforter. She then transferred the woman to the bed, removed her shoes, assisted her back against the pillow and covered her with a light blanket. Next she ran a practiced gaze over the night table, which, she saw, held a full carafe of water with a matching small glass, a box of tissues and a ceramic bell. Beside the bell was a book.

"Do you use reading glasses?" Claire asked. "If you do, I don't see them."

"No."

Claire's gaze went back to her charge. She would have liked to take a proper reading of the older woman's vital signs, but her equipment was still packed, and she doubted Mae Parker would agree to wait until she got what she needed. "Is there anything else I can do to make you more comfortable?" When the matriarch shook her head, Claire added softly, "Then I'll be in the next room."

She'd gone only a few steps before the woman stopped her.

"Well, what are you gonna do?" she demanded. "Stay or leave?"

Claire turned around. If she thought Mae Parker had faked her collapse, she'd leave. But she didn't.

"I'll stay," she said.

"And you mean it this time?"

"I mean it," Claire confirmed.

"Good," the woman said, and closed her eyes. "You won't regret it."

THOSE LAST WORDS ECHOED in Claire's mind as she settled to wait in a comfortable chair in the parlor. They'd been meant as reassurance—a promise, even. But Claire had learned long ago not to put faith in promises. All too often they were forgotten, or never meant in the first place. Life was easier when taken one minute, one hour at a time.

She wished Mae Parker well, as she did all her patients. She'd give her the best care she could render. But the woman would be no different from the other patients Claire had cared for over the years. When her services were no longer warranted she'd leave this place in the same state as she'd arrived—her emotions intact.

Because that was a lesson she'd also learned a long time ago. *She* was the only person she had to rely on.

CHAPTER TWO

THE PARKERS WHO REMAINED in the dining room after Mae's startling exit were uncharacteristically silent.

Tanner, aware of his outsider status, cleared his throat. "Maybe this is where I should say adios. You folks don't need a visitor now, particularly one that riles Mae every time she looks at him. I'll repack my things and head back to Phoenix."

"No, don't," Rafe said shortly.

"But I came for a specific purpose, and it's something Mae's dead set against."

Rafe threw him a hard look. "She'll be even more upset if you leave. You heard her. She's always been a stickler for treatin' you kids right."

"I haven't been a 'kid' for over twenty years."

"Rafe's right." Shannon backed up her husband, her blue eyes still wide with shock. "It would only make matters worse."

"Maybe you should ease off on the computer thing for a while, though, Rafe," Harriet urged. "Since Mae— Since she—"

"A nurse!" Rafe repeated his earlier incredulity.

"Who'da thought Aunt Mae would *do* somethin' like that?" LeRoy said, shaking his head.

Shannon's gaze moved from one to the other. "Did you see the way Marie looked at her? I'm sure she thinks Mae's hired a nurse because it took so long for someone to find her the day she fell."

"Surely she wouldn't think that!" Harriet exclaimed.

Shannon shrugged. "Maybe Mae blames us, too."

Harriet grew paler. "She said it's because we're so busy."

Then LeRoy put into words what the others must have been thinking, because no one broke the resulting silence.

"Just how bad do you think Aunt Mae *is?*"

TANNER MOVED WITH THE men onto the front porch after the women said they would wait a few minutes, then go check on Mae. Once outside, the talk turned to the safer topics of weather and ranching. Tanner listened as the two cousins speculated about the prospects for the fall roundup after a drier than normal spring, a continuing rainless early summer and forecasts that didn't offer much encouragement for the coming months.

The huge ranch, numbering into the hundreds of

sections, had been in the Parker family for generations, going back to the area's first settlers. The present-day family worked it in much the same way as their ancestors—traditionally, with a man on a horse tending cattle that were as good as wild when they were collected twice a year from the mesas, canyons and sweeping valleys. The Parkers were a breed apart—tough, hardy, with the steellike will to do what they thought was right.

The first time Tanner had met them after his widowed father married Rafe's widowed mother, they'd seemed larger than life. To his young eyes they were awesome. Especially Rafe, his new stepbrother. Rafe had been heir-apparent to manage the ranch then, though he'd yet to turn twenty. Mae had been acting manager. She'd been as tough as old boots and fiercely determined, always demanding that those around her do her bidding. She still did. But now that her health had started to deteriorate, the members of her clan—usually so formidable—were shaken. The men didn't show it in overt ways, but their deep concern was evident to anyone who knew them.

As the weather-and-ranch conversation carried on, Tanner leaned against the porch railing and gazed at the grassy courtyard rimmed by the compound's five houses. Four houses, low to the ground with long narrow porches and red tile roofs, faced one another, two by two, across the long arms of a U-shaped drive. The fifth house, this one, was a two-story structure with a stone facade and twin porches of handsomely carved black wrought iron. As the main house, it dominated the others in size as well as placement.

Tanner remembered the first time he'd seen the place when he was a boy of ten. His imagination had already been captured by the stories his new mother had told about Mae and the Parkers—

Rafe clapped him on the back, jolting him from the past.

"You shouldn't take any of this personally, you know, Tanner. Mae's just recently come around to usin' a telephone without thinking someone's listenin' in. Remember how she used to avoid 'em like the plague? Had Gib take her everywhere?"

Gib Parker was uncle to both Rafe and LeRoy.

"She sure did," LeRoy confirmed.

As always when he was in the company of his stepbrother, Tanner wished he'd had more of an opportunity over the years to know Rafe better. Mae's ongoing disapproval of what she considered the too hasty marriage between their parents had made that all but impossible. He could count on the fingers of one hand the number of his visits to the ranch—including the last, which had been Rafe's marriage to Shannon eleven years earlier.

The entire Reid family had attended the huge affair and had been treated with the utmost courtesy. That was Mae's way. From the beginning she'd refused to attach blame to the Reid children for what she considered the wrongdoing of the adults. She'd extended invitations for the youngsters to visit the ranch, and those who'd accepted even stayed in her house. But the strain remained in force between Gloria, Rafe's mother, and Mae. At the wedding it was clear that Mae continued to carry a grudge against Gloria for acting contrary to her wishes, and Gloria, happy in her second marriage, remained totally unrepentant.

"Aunt Mae'll come around to havin' you work on the records," Rafe assured him, breaking into his thoughts again.

Without knowing it, though, Rafe repeated the same optimistic view Gloria had given her five new stepchildren all those years before—an optimism Tanner now doubted would ever be justified.

Rafe continued, "There's no use holding on to the old ways when new ones are so much better. I've seen what Jim Cleary's new manager's done with his records." He referred to the owner of the nearest neighboring ranch. "Sure beats the old index cards we use to heck and back. You get done with the paperwork so much faster and can keep run of things easier. Aunt Mae'll come around," he repeated, "just as soon as she gets a chance to see for herself what modernization can do for us." Rafe leaned back to look at him. "You don't have any place you have to be for the next few weeks, do you?"

Tanner thought of his suddenly aimless state. He had nowhere he had to be at any time. Some would think that must be heaven. But not when you were accustomed to working eighty-hour weeks. He didn't know what to do with himself. Or if he even *wanted* to do anything. It was that—the not wanting—that had caused Gloria such concern. It was so out of character for him. Barely a week after his return to Phoenix from northern California, he'd overheard her on the phone to Rafe recommending his services. "It's the natural solution to everything! Tanner knows all about computers," she'd proclaimed proudly.

Tanner straightened from the railing. "Nowhere in particular, no," he said.

Rafe's slow smile spread. "Then why not do what Mae says and consider this a vacation? That way you'll be handy when she comes around to agreein' with what I want to do. Can't have you off somewhere startin' another software company. We might not get you back."

LeRoy entered into the teasing. "Never woulda believed I'd be standin' so close to one of them

there computer moguls we hear so much about.''
He surveyed Tanner from head to toe. ''Don't look
all that different. No bulgin' head or twirly eyes or
anythin'!''

Tanner had been on the receiving end of cowboy
humor before when he'd visited the ranch. He
knew that his best option was to go along with it,
or the kidding would only get worse. ''The term's
geeks, LeRoy. Computer geeks.''

''Do they have twirly eyes?'' LeRoy demanded.

''Sometimes.'' Tanner laughed. ''When there's
a deadline to meet.''

''At least when you're ridin' a horse, you can
get off it,'' Rafe chimed in. ''Damn computers
don't sound like they'd be any fun to saddle!''

''There've been times when I wouldn't've
minded having some spurs,'' Tanner quipped.

Both men laughed, leaving Tanner with a warm
feeling. The family had always treated him well,
but he'd never felt that he measured up in their
eyes. The Parkers didn't know him well enough in
the ways that counted to them to decide that. During the two-week summer vacations he and his
brother had spent at the ranch, they'd been treated
as guests. They'd never worked cattle or fixed
fence.

This was the perfect opportunity to change that.
He could spend some of his suddenly limitless free

time to get to know these people, to let them know him. To show them, as well as himself, that he could win their valued approval. They were part of his life, past and present. At least, such as his life was after the blur of the past few years, the past few months, the past few terrible weeks—

"We'll find you some real spurs," Rafe said. "Then we'll see how you take to ridin' again."

"I was fifteen the last time I was on a horse."

"You won't forget. I seem to remember you never embarrassed yourself."

Tanner chuckled. "I didn't fall off it, you mean."

"No, better than that. You were actually pretty good."

Three children ran up the drive and onto the porch, their boots clomping on the sound oak boards. Both boys were junior replicas of Rafe, the same dark hair, dark eyes and features that were strong even in a seven- and an eight-year-old. The girl, slightly older, was LeRoy's daughter. Her mass of black curls bounced as she ran. A yellow dog was close on her heels.

"Daddy! We wanna go look for gold!" Nate, the younger of the two boys, blurted out.

Ward, the older boy, sent him a withering look before trying a more mature approach. "Wes says he'll take us tomorrow mornin' if it's okay with you, Daddy. It's been a long time since we've been out to Red Canyon, and you said we could go again soon.''

Rafe met LeRoy's eyes in a gleam of remembered excitement. The missing gold coins had been lost by one of their ancestors after a cattle drive in the late 1800s, and each generation of Parker children had taken a turn searching for them ever since. Tanner had even looked for them once himself as a boy. To this day, the ''prize'' remained elusive.

''That's fine by me,'' Rafe drawled easily, then, over the childish whoops, added, ''but only if your mother agrees. You, too, LeRoy?''

LeRoy looked down at his daughter Anna, who'd flung her arms around his waist. ''Sure, same for me,'' he said fondly.

The children made a dash for the door.

''Don't—'' Rafe began, only to have the screen door slam shut before he could finish. He winced.

''In the old days Mae woulda come boilin' out, fussin' up a storm when she heard that door slam,'' LeRoy mused.

''In the old days, she wouldn't've been in bed so early.''

A glum silence settled between the two cousins as they once again contemplated the matriarch's increasing vulnerability.

"Whatcha think of that nurse?" LeRoy asked eventually.

"She doesn't say much," Rafe replied.

"Think we should get Tate to run a check on her?" LeRoy asked, referring to the local sheriff and husband of their younger cousin, Jodie.

"You see somethin' you don't like?" Rafe asked him quickly.

"Not really." LeRoy shrugged. "It's just all happened kinda sudden."

Tanner was well aware that he had no standing in the family. Still, he felt compelled to offer an opinion. "She seemed okay to me."

A smile creased LeRoy's cheeks. "So, you think she's kinda cute, huh?"

"I wouldn't say *cute*. She's more—"

Tanner had been going to say *interesting-looking*, but the boys burst back through the screen door, though this time they were careful not to let it bang shut.

"Mom says yes!" Nate cried, again the first to herald the news. "But we hafta clean our rooms up."

"Where's Anna?" LeRoy asked.

Ward frowned. "She was right behind us."

"I'm here," Anna said primly, pushing through the door. "Mama said not to run, so I didn't."

Ward rolled his eyes. "They said we hafta get

our rooms done tonight. Before bed. So we gotta hurry!''

''Hurry!'' Nate agreed exuberantly.

His older brother gave him another withering look. ''Your side of the room's a lot messier than mine.''

''Mine's not as bad as Anna's!'' Nate defended.

''My room's not messy!'' Anna cried.

''Shouldn't y'all stop wastin' so much time?'' Rafe chided them.

The children were down the steps and at the end of the short walkway in a flash. They divided at the hard-packed gravel drive—the girl running to the house farthest on the right, and the boys running to the nearest house on the left.

The yellow Labrador, Junior, had been occupying himself snuffling around the flower beds. As the children scampered away, he seemed confused as to who to follow. He looked one way, then the other, until Rafe called to him. Then he trooped onto the porch and settled contentedly in a spot not far from Tanner's feet.

Tanner reached down to rub the dog's ears and, for his effort, received a warm lick. He looked up to find Rafe watching them. The normal intensity of his stepbrother's gaze had softened to the point where Tanner couldn't help but wonder if Rafe was thinking of another yellow dog who'd once

called the ranch home. Rafe's beloved cowdog,
Shep—the namesake for Shep, Jr., now just Junior.
For some reason during Tanner's brief summer visits, Shep had latched on to him and followed him
almost everywhere he went. The favoritism was
obvious enough for Tanner to worry that Rafe
might resent it. But then, as now, Rafe wasn't an-
noyed. Instead, he seemed to hold his dog's judgment in high regard.

LeRoy grinned. "Wonder if anyone's ever
gonna find those old coins? Parker kids have dug
more holes lookin' for 'em over the years. Good
thing our daddies made us fill 'em in. Otherwise,
parts of the ranch would look like the moon!"

"Mae told me once she remembered hearin' her
daddy and his brothers talk about it," Rafe said.

"She's dug her fair share, too," LeRoy remarked.

"Sure she did," Rafe agreed, and once again the
pair grew silent as they thought of the elderly
woman who for so long had been the family's driving force.

Tanner had to look away. His best friend and
partner's unexpected death was still too close for
him not to react to the foreboding of the others.
Granted, there was a huge difference between the
decline of a person who had lived a long and rewarding life and the sudden demise of a young

vibrant man who had recently realized everything he'd—they'd—been working for so diligently.

To cover his fragile emotions, Tanner again reached to rub Junior's ears.

CLAIRE WAS LEAFING THROUGH a magazine she'd discovered in the parlor when someone knocked lightly on the door. Within a second a crack appeared and a blond head peeped through.

"How is she?" Shannon asked softly.

"She's napping," Claire replied, and put the magazine aside.

Shannon exchanged whispers with someone behind her, then looked again at Claire. "Could we talk…out here?"

When Claire stepped into the hall she found Shannon and Harriet, their features tight with worry. To alleviate some of their concern, she offered, "It's only natural that a person your aunt's age will be slowing down. And that she could have what she terms 'spells.'"

"Spells?" Shannon repeated the word, frowning. "You make it sound as if she's had more than the two we know about."

"The one in the bathtub and the one just now," Harriet clarified.

Too late Claire realized that she might have divulged privileged information.

The women obviously had the same thought and looked at each other.

"That would go a long way to explaining why she's suddenly hired—" Shannon paused "—Claire… isn't that your name?"

"Claire Hannaford, yes," Claire confirmed.

"When did she first contact you, Claire?" Harriet demanded. "What did she say?"

Shannon hastened to explain. "We know all this must seem over-the-top to you. But for Mae to hire a nurse…then to collapse the way she did." She took a steadying breath. "If we seem a little… intense, it's because we've all been knocked off balance. We've pleaded with her to let us help, but she's refused. Then, out of the blue, she presents us with you!"

"I work through an agency in Midland. You're welcome to contact them if you have doubts about my competency."

"It's not *you*," Shannon denied. "It's Mae! We've always— She's always— If you'd met her before, you'd—" She turned anxiously to Harriet. "What are we going to do? You know how Mae feels about doctors. She'll barely let Dr. Stevens look at her, and she *likes* him."

"Have you spoken to her doctor?" Harriet asked Claire quickly.

"Not yet," Claire said. "The doctor normally brings me to a case. But in this instance, your aunt made all the arrangements herself."

"When?" Harriet pressed.

"The day before yesterday, Friday."

"Isn't that typical?" Shannon muttered in exasperation. "Mae makes up her mind to do something, and—"

"What's *typical?*" The matriarch of the family stood in the now open doorway. "What are you three doin'? Gossipin' about me? 'Cause if that's what it is, I'll tell you right now I'm fine. All I needed was a little rest."

Shannon reached solicitously for her arm. "Mae, do you think you should be up so soon?"

"Of course, I should." Mae evaded her grasp. "Now, get out of the way so I can get that coffee I missed out on."

The women's beseeching gazes turned on Claire. They silently pleaded for her to tell them if the elderly woman was as well as she claimed. Claire performed a quick survey of the Parker family matriarch, who returned her scrutiny with a look of fierce independence. Some color was back in her cheeks and no sign of her previous weakness remained.

"Miss Parker," Claire said after a moment, "if

you don't mind, I won't accompany you. It's been a very long day.''

Her answer startled the other two women, but pleased her patient.

''Do what you like,'' Mae said gruffly, then set off down the hall, the tip of her cane tapping determinedly on the gray stone floor.

''We'll talk later,'' Shannon said hurriedly, and still looking slightly dazed, she moved to catch up with Harriet...who was trying to catch up with Mae.

Claire watched until the three women reached the end of the hall, then stepped back into the parlor and took a deep breath.

This was not going to be an easy assignment.

The Parkers were completely different from the families she was accustomed to. Most of her previous clients had been forgotten by their ''nearest and dearest,'' or else the relatives showed up only when it was too late.

She didn't know what to make of the Parkers...of their brand of family dynamics.

What a person doesn't have, they don't miss.

Claire could hear Mrs. Stanton's kind voice repeat the words.

Mrs. Stanton had come into her life several times during her younger years. She'd cared for Claire as an infant, then later—on occasion—

reprised her role as a temporary foster mom when problems arose in Claire's assigned homes.

Make the best of each situation. Treat others as you want to be treated.

Claire hadn't seen her beyond her twelfth birthday.

What a person doesn't have...

Claire resettled in the chair she'd vacated minutes before and reached again for her magazine. She soon became absorbed in an article that she guessed was typical ranch fare—the dangers of a fire ant infestation to a herd of cattle.

CHAPTER THREE

CLAIRE AWAKENED THE NEXT morning to the sound of gentle snores coming from the adjoining room. She yawned, stretched, then scooted a little way up the narrow bed.

The first object her gaze alighted on was the wardrobe trunk Axel had delivered the evening before. His bald head had shone as he'd supported it on his bowed shoulders and back. Claire had protested; she hadn't wanted him to hurt himself. She usually brought the drawers and hanging clothes inside in several trips, then dragged the empty trunk. But in a surprisingly thin voice for a man his size, he'd made light of the weight before shifting the burden onto the rug. Afterward, he'd bearhugged it to an out-of-the-way spot before again relinquishing the room to her.

Claire's offer to help Mae Parker prepare for bed upon her return from her delayed coffee had also been met with similar resistance.

"You're not on the clock yet," the matriarch

had said. "Get some rest." And even though it was barely nine o'clock, Claire had done as instructed. She'd already used the time while Mae was away to perform her brand of settling in—setting out her needed toilet articles, her nurse's kit and a few of her favorite keepsakes, but keeping everything else intact, as was her usual habit.

Her sleep had been unbroken, which meant her charge had also spent an undisturbed night.

A snore broke off in midrasp, followed by a disjointed murmur.

Claire slipped into her robe and padded into the other room.

"Good morning," she said pleasantly as she saw the elderly woman push herself upright in the double bed. "Would you like me to draw your bath? Or do you prefer to wake slowly with coffee and a newspaper?"

Mae Parker looked fierce even in the morning. Her features were as stern as at their first meeting; her gaze just as sharp. The only softening note was her thinning white hair, released for the night from the tautly held topknot and falling in long wisps onto the shoulders of her tailored pajamas.

She nodded toward the bedside chair. "Why don't you sit down so we can talk."

Claire took a moment to adjust the pillow behind

her charge's back, making sure it supported her properly, before she settled in the proffered seat.

"I've told you before I'm not helpless!" Mae snapped crossly.

"I know."

"I don't like havin' things done for me that I can do myself!"

"You have a housekeeper," Claire reminded her.

"I don't like keepin' house!" The woman's annoyance lessened as she examined Claire. "How'd you sleep last night? Bed all right? We can change it if we need to. Axel can—"

"It was fine. I slept like a baby."

"I saw when I came in that you'd unpacked a few things. So you really *are* plannin' to stick around?"

"I said I would."

"Can't always depend on what people say."

Claire hadn't planned to test the waters so soon, but she needed to know her situation. "Is that why you hired a nurse? Because you can't depend on your family?"

Mae Parker looked shocked. "I trust my family with my life!"

"I ask because they say they want to care for you, and you won't allow it."

"I won't *allow* it because I don't want to be a burden!"

Despite the fact that the woman's dark eyes bored into her, Claire persevered. "They don't seem to think of you as a burden."

"Are you *tryin'* to talk yourself out of a job?"

The housekeeper chose that moment to sweep into the room, carrying a bed tray.

At the sight of it, Mae's expression tightened even more.

"Oh, you're here," the woman said flatly, glancing at Claire. "There's only enough coffee for Miss Parker."

"What are you doin', Marie, bringin' me coffee?" Mae demanded.

The housekeeper placed the tray over her employer's lap, her voice warming. "I've brought some toast and jelly for you, too. In case you're hungry."

"I always have breakfast in the dining room."

The housekeeper seemed oblivious to the warning signals. She smiled as she straightened. "No reason you can't have a treat."

"A treat!" Mae exploded. "Here, take this thing." She thrust the tray back into the housekeeper's hands.

The woman's smile finally faltered. "But I thought—"

"Well, don't!" Mae snapped. Then, at the housekeeper's crestfallen look, she moderated her irritation. "It was a kind thought, but I don't need it. I'll be in the dining room in a half hour, like I always am. Claire and I *both* will be there."

Marie sent Claire a resentful look that prompted Mae to shake her head.

"I never thought I'd see the day when a guest on this ranch would be treated so badly. I'm disappointed in you, Marie. Truly disappointed."

Marie flushed bright red and apologized stiffly, "I'm sorry."

Mae relented again. "I've told you. You and Axel can look after me as good as you always have. But I'm not willin' to put all the extra work on you, just like I'm not willin' to put it on the others."

"I wouldn't mind," Marie answered tightly.

"I know you wouldn't."

The housekeeper sniffed, then with a furtive glance at Claire, she hurried from the room, taking the tray with her.

Mae sighed once they were alone. "That's the hardest thing about gettin' old—havin' to say goodbye to your friends."

Claire had known the woman for barely one day, but such a negative outlook didn't seem a part of her personality. She frowned. "Miss Parker...I'm sure you still have a good deal of time left to—"

Mae cut in. "When it's just the two of us, let's stick to the truth, all right? That's the real reason I brought an outsider to the ranch. Can't say things like that to the family. They get too upset. I *know* my time's comin'. I can feel it! But there's still too many things that need doin'...things I'm goin' to be needin' your help with."

"You mean...writing letters, sorting through your personal possessions?"

"Somethin' like that," Mae agreed.

Claire did her best to probe behind the steady black gaze because she sensed the woman was holding something important back, but she got nowhere. Mae Parker was a pro at keeping her thoughts to herself.

Finally, belatedly, she said, "Of course," and was rewarded with another faint satisfied smile.

A HALF HOUR LATER THE TWO women sat in the dining room. Breakfast had been served, but under such strained conditions that Claire knew she would soon have to meet privately with the housekeeper. There had to be a way to convince Marie that Claire wasn't a threat to her position in the household.

To Claire's relief, Mae Parker made no further

criticisms of the housekeeper's actions, and shortly
after finishing her cereal and toast, she pushed
away from the table, announcing that she would be
in her office for the next hour. Since she made no
suggestion that Claire accompany her, Claire knew
she was on her own. A perfect opportunity to talk
with Marie.

She'd just reached for a final sip of coffee when
the housekeeper marched into the room and
whisked the cup away.

"You're done with that," she stated pugna-
ciously, and turned on her heels to disappear back
into the kitchen.

Claire stared after her, stunned. The woman
wanted her to follow and complain. She'd be waiting in the next room, both barrels at the ready. Not
the atmosphere Claire thought most conducive for
their private talk.

Instead of falling in with the housekeeper's
plans, she returned to the bedroom parlor, hoping
that a short delay would dampen the woman's boil-
ing resentment. To pass a little time, she made her
bed and straightened the area around it, mindful
not to encroach on any of Marie's usual morning
duties in Mae's room.

When she finished, the parlor looked much as it
had on her arrival, with the exception of her an-
tique trunk. Claire had acquired the unusual piece

of luggage shortly after turning eighteen, when the client from her first home help job had given it to her. The woman had been a dancer in vaudeville reviews and had taken the trunk to all her play dates. She'd insisted that Claire accept it, confident that she would grow to love it as much as she herself did.

Claire smiled as she touched one of the time-worn transit patches that still spotted the exterior. She did love it, just as she loved the small mementos she'd collected through the years and kept tucked inside. In effect, the trunk held her life.

She couldn't help but wonder at the housekeeper's reaction when she'd first seen it. Worn and battered, the trunk didn't fit the decor of the parlor, not even in the room's hybrid state. Did it cause the housekeeper the same irritation as Claire herself did?

Claire glanced at her watch. Enough time had passed.

She took a deep breath and headed toward the kitchen.

MARIE STOOD AT THE SINK, her broad back to the door. She was unable to see that Claire had slipped into the room.

"Smart little thing she thinks she is," the housekeeper fumed as she peeled a mound of potatoes.

"Comin' here, expectin' to be treated like a guest. A guest! We all know she'll be cashin' her paychecks just like we do!"

Axel had been resting his considerable bulk on a corner stool, and he spotted Claire the instant she came in. "Marie—" he cautioned, tensing.

Deep in her own aggrieved thoughts, the housekeeper continued to grumble. "I can certainly take better care of Miss Mae than she ever could! I know the woman. I know what she likes and doesn't like. What she needs. How long have we been here, you and me, Axel? Over thirty years, that's how long, and it should *mean* somethin'!"

Axel slid off the stool to catch hold of his wife and turn her around.

Marie fended him off. "What in tarnation are you doin', Axel Douglas? Are you tryin' to drive me nuts? You know I'm as mad as all get out, yet you—"

Then she spotted Claire, and another rush of blood suffused her face.

Claire forced a smile. She should have made some kind of sound to announce her presence. The housekeeper was sure to add this humiliation to the list of her other offenses.

Axel, grinning broadly, rushed to pump her hand. "We weren't introduced properly last night, were we? I'm Axel...Axel Douglas, and this here's my wife, Marie. I'm the camp cook in these parts. Fix the meals for the cowboys each and every day. Do the same on roundups. Marie here keeps things straight in the main house…but I s'pose you already know that.''

"Axel, stop it!" Marie hissed, her embarrassment deepening.

Her husband dropped Claire's hand and backed away, his smile dimming as he rubbed his palms on the sides of his jeans.

"I was wondering if I might have a glass of tea?" Claire asked, inventing an excuse for being there. "Water would be fine, though. I'm not picky."

Marie made a show of rinsing and drying her hands before filling a glass with water. Only, she made no attempt at delivery. She held it extended instead. If Claire wanted the glass, she would have to come get it.

Claire sighed to herself and crossed the space between them. If placating the woman would get them on better footing—

She took a sip before easing away a few steps. "That's very good, thanks."

"Just water," Marie replied, and turned back to the sink.

Claire glanced at Axel, who looked just as uncomfortable as she felt.

"Are those for lunch?" she asked, motioning to the growing mound of peeled potatoes.

He nodded. "Marie's makin' her extra-special vegetable soup. Miss Jodie's been known to drive all the way from Del Norte when she hears it's bein' served."

"Jodie?" Claire repeated the name for something to say.

"She's another Parker...well, Connelly now. She's ole Mae's great-niece. Married to Tate Connelly. He's the sheriff of Briggs County. *This* is Brig—"

"Axel!" Marie dropped the peeler and spun around. "She's not interested in what county we live in!" She fixed Claire with a hostile glare. "What is it you really want? It sure wasn't water!" She motioned to the still full glass.

Claire stopped all pretense and set the glass on the counter. "I'd like to talk to you," she answered quietly.

"What about?" the housekeeper demanded.

"About me. Being here."

Marie narrowed her eyes. "I'm not the one to talk to about that."

Undaunted, Claire plunged on. "I'm not here to take over your duties...or to interfere in any way with your relationship with Miss Parker. I'm only here to do the job I was hired to do. It's as simple as that."

The housekeeper wasn't convinced. "You don't need special trainin' to look after a person. You just need to care about 'em."

"Sometimes it takes more than that," Claire disagreed. "When a person's ill—"

"She's *not* ill!"

Claire tried again. "When a person begins to go down physically—"

"Don't *say* things like that!" Marie burst out, and grabbing the dish towel, she lunged at Claire, brandishing it like a weapon. "Not in my kitchen! Miss Parker's fine…just fine! And if you think different, you can—"

Axel inserted himself into his wife's path and caught hold of her shoulders. "You're goin' overboard, woman!" he chastised her.

Marie looked blankly at him, at the dish towel, then crumpled against him. "Make her stop sayin' that, Axel," she moaned into his shirt. "Mae's not goin' downhill. She's still just as strong, just as cantankerous, just as *wonderful* as she's always been!"

Axel's large hands stroked his wife's short hair. He spoke soothingly to her. "You know she's gettin' older. There's no denyin' it. And she's the one who's brought this young lady here. It's what *she* wants. Best thing we can do is accept it.''

Claire, who had instinctively shrunk from the housekeeper's aggression, watched as the man comforted his distraught wife. Her presence at the ranch was causing such dismay. No one wanted to believe that Mae Parker's health might be in decline. What surprised Claire most, though, was the magnitude of the affection they all seemed to feel for the woman.

Such deep affection made Claire uneasy. She'd worked hard to keep herself from ever again being in such a situation. And although her emotions were not involved this time, it reminded her too vividly of what she'd once been through.

She backed toward the door.

Not understanding the reason for her retreat, Axel tried to reassure her. ''Marie won't hurt ya. She's just upset. Ole Mae means a lot to her.''

''Of course she does,'' Claire whispered.

Sobs shook the housekeeper's shoulders as she burrowed her face deeper into her husband's chest. ''It's all…my fault,'' she cried brokenly. ''Miss Mae blames me!''

She had to get away, Claire thought. She had to break free of these agitated feelings in order to maintain her trademark tranquility.

With her eyes on the floor, she hurried out of the kitchen. Then through the living room into the entryway. Only to stop just in time to keep from running into someone. The *real* guest at the Parker Ranch.

"What's this?" the man she knew only as Tanner demanded.

"I'm sorry," Claire apologized, and tried to go around him.

He stepped in her way. "No, seriously, what's happened?" He ducked down from his healthy six feet to examine her. "You're upset. Ah!" His expression cleared as he glanced back toward the kitchen. "You've tangled with Marie! She didn't seem very pleased to see you last night. For as long as I've known her, she's considered herself the Keeper at the Parker Gate. The Guardian Dragon." He grinned and added confidingly, "Sometimes she breathes fire."

Claire was not in the mood for teasing. Especially teasing at her expense. "*Everyone* here breathes fire," she retorted.

"Not me. I'm Tanner—Tanner Reid. You probably don't remember, because who can remember much of anything when you're first introduced to the Parkers. They kind of overwhelm you. I'm not one of them. I'm Rafe's stepbrother from Arizona.

Rafe…the ranch manager?'' When she nodded jerkily, he continued, ''I arrived the day before you did, and I'm not exactly welcome, either. At least, not as far as Mae's concerned.'' He grinned again. ''And of the two…I'd rather have Marie upset with me than Mae!''

The door to Mae's office opened, and the matriarch set her black cane tapping toward them.

''What's this?'' she demanded as she drew close.

''I'm flirting with your nurse,'' Tanner claimed, and winked at Claire for a second time, only more blatantly than on the previous night.

''Well, leave her alone,'' Mae commanded as she took in Claire's unsettled state.

Claire didn't want her new employer to think that he was the cause of her upset. ''He's not bothering me,'' Claire denied hastily. Then she realized she couldn't explain the true reason for her distress. ''He's just— I— He was telling me about the ranch.''

Mae tilted her head. ''Then why not have him show it to you instead? Tanner, take her down to the work area. Let her see what the heart of a real working ranch looks like. You know your way around well enough to explain most things. Show her the ranch office, too. She should know where it is…where everything is.'' Mae surveyed his clothing, which today consisted of a pair of worn jeans, a faded western shirt and, incongruously, athletic shoes. ''That is, unless you've already got somethin' planned.''

Tanner looked down at himself rather sheepishly. ''Rafe's loaned me a few of his things. But I need to buy some boots.''

''Get 'em in Del Norte,'' Mae said quickly. ''Take Claire with you there, too. For the same reason.''

Claire spoke up. The situation had gotten out of hand. ''Miss Parker, I'm here to help *you*.''

''And you'll be doin' that by gettin' your bearings! A few hours won't—''

Mae stopped, her attention jumping to a point beyond Claire's shoulder.

Turning in the same direction, Claire saw that Marie and Axel had come to stand in the living room. The housekeeper's face was mottled, her eyes damp.

''—be a problem,'' Mae continued, as if there'd been no interruption. ''Marie'll be here to watch out for me, won't you, Marie?''

''I sure will!'' The housekeeper's emphatic confirmation ended on a sniff, which caused her husband to tighten his arm around her shoulders.

"I'd really rather not..." Claire began, but at the same time Mae issued another command.

"Have her back by two o'clock, Tanner." Then the older woman brushed past them on her way to the porch.

The four people left behind were silent until Tanner shrugged and said to Claire, "Looks like we're going to Del Norte."

"I don't want to," Claire reiterated.

Marie swelled up indignantly. "And why not? I've been watchin' out for Miss Parker for more years than you've been alive! I think I can manage to do it again for a few hours!"

"Now, Marie—" Axel cautioned his wife, and to prevent more trouble, he hustled her back into the kitchen.

The housekeeper's continuing vexation carried through the closed door.

Tanner looked at Claire. "And where did you say you'd like to start? The ranch...or town?"

"Give me five minutes," Claire said crisply, and slipping around him, headed for the parlor.

CLAIRE COULD REORDER herself in minutes. All she had to do was be on her own, relax, clear her mind, take a few deep breaths and....

This time the process didn't work.

Something about this place—these people—interfered.

She should have listened to her first instinct and turned the assignment down. She'd had *two* opportunities. Now, she had to make the best of it.

But just what, exactly, had she let herself in for?

CHAPTER FOUR

TANNER ACCOMPANIED THE newcomer down the path toward the working heart of the Parker Ranch. She'd said nothing beyond a murmured reply to his greeting since they'd met up again in the entryway.

He glanced at her from the corner of his eye, curious about what she might be thinking. Her expression was composed, noncommittal. He looked away, then back again, this time with more masculine interest.

As LeRoy had said, she was cute. She had a rounded face and slightly squared jaw, with wide-spaced smoke-colored eyes and a feathery fringe of light brown hair. That she didn't reach to the top of his shoulder had surprised him. Last night he'd thought she was taller. Slim and delicately built, she had a certain fey quality, as if she wasn't quite…real.

In an attempt to get her to talk, he said, "So…you take care of people for a living."

"Yes," she replied briefly.

"How long have you been doing it?"

She gave him a penetrating look, then began a recitation. "I've been in home health care for ten years, since I turned eighteen. I earned my LVN certificate—LVN is short for Licensed Vocational Nurse—when I turned twenty-two. You, or any of the Parkers, are welcome to call the school I attended, and if you like, I can provide you with references for—"

The litany stopped when she saw his slow grin.

"I was just trying to make conversation," he explained.

Her gray eyes didn't waver. "Why?"

"The Parkers tend to circle the wagons when something happens they don't like. If you're one of them, great. If you're not...they can be hard to deal with. I thought, since we're both outsiders—"

"I came here to do a job, Mr. Reid, not socialize."

Tanner smiled. "Who's socializing? I'm just following orders like you are. And call me Tanner," he invited.

She turned her head away.

They continued on in silence until they reached the spot where they needed to veer off to the right.

Tanner motioned in that direction. "The garage is over there, next to the barn. I thought we'd go to town first, get that out of the way, then look around here when we get back.''

''All right,'' she agreed shortly.

He pulled to a sudden stop, tired of her cool treatment. ''Hey! Like I said, I'm only following orders. I'm not the one making you do what you don't want to do.''

She stopped as well. ''I don't exactly have a winning position here, do I? If I don't go, Miss Parker will be displeased and Marie will see it as an additional insult. If I do—'' She rubbed the skin between her nicely formed eyebrows.

''You'll have to put up with me.''

She frowned in frustration. ''This is so different from the way I normally start a job. Running off the first day to sightsee!''

''Mae told you to do it.''

''It's not the way *I* do things.''

Tanner cocked his head. The few women he'd spent his rare off-hours with over the past few years had known how to have a good time. A serious woman concerned about *her* job was something new. ''You don't like disruptions, do you?'' he probed curiously.

''I'll tell Miss Parker I have a headache,'' she said, spinning around to retrace her steps to the main house. ''It won't be that much of a lie.''

Tanner caught hold of her arm and was surprised

by his reaction to her warm, soft flesh. "I didn't mean to be rude. I was just— Do you think we could start over with this? I'd *like* to show you around. And it seems important to Mae that you know your way." He added humorously, "I promise I won't be too obnoxious."

She remained rigid for a moment, then the tension in her arm relaxed.

"All right," she said at last, "I'll go."

He flashed a smile, but she swiftly looked away.

THE EVENING BEFORE, Claire had left her little car on the U-shaped drive in front of the main house. By morning, it had disappeared. She found it parked in the long garage, alongside two other cars—a black Cadillac and a new blue BMW with the top down. The far side of the garage supported what amounted to a professional mechanic's work area, complete with a small pit and a hydraulic lift. LeRoy, dressed in coveralls, uncoiled himself from beneath the hood of a pale green pickup.

"You two off to town?" he asked, using a rag to wipe oil and grease from his hands. "Axel stopped by on his way to the cook house to tell me you were comin'. I checked your tires, Tanner. Figured you'd want to take your new car out for a spin."

"Sure doesn't take long for word to spread around here," Tanner said.

"Nope." LeRoy's dark gaze twinkled at Claire. "Good mornin', Miss Hannaford."

"Good morning, Mr. Parker." Claire made herself smile as well.

"The last name's Dunn," LeRoy corrected jovially. "I'm a Parker through my mom. Takes a while to sort everyone out. But don't worry. We'll keep you straight until you do."

Tanner ran a loving hand over the trunk of the sporty blue convertible.

"Must be fun to drive," LeRoy said, watching him.

"Try it yourself whenever you like."

LeRoy grinned. "Thanks, I might just do that. Always wondered how one a' these fancy little things would feel."

Tanner opened the passenger door and glanced expectantly at Claire. Though nothing about this excursion felt right to her, she settled into the low bucket seat.

Once he got behind the wheel, she shifted as close to the window as she could, but the car's compact interior forced an intimacy she didn't want. All she could do was fold her hands in her lap and cling to her professionalism.

LeRoy waved them away onto the narrow road

that skirted the corrals, then watched as they connected with the wider road leading from ranch headquarters.

After a few miles she asked, "Your car is new?"

He nodded. "I got it a couple of weeks ago."

"It's…very nice."

"Yeah," he agreed.

Claire glanced at him. He'd become very quiet after getting in the car. And from the way he'd answered her, she sensed some deep regret mixed in with his pride of ownership. "Aren't you happy with it?" she asked.

The question seemed to startle him. He turned to her briefly. "Why do you ask that?"

"Because you don't act as if you're happy."

"I love this car," he claimed. "It's the car I've always wanted!"

"I didn't mean to upset you."

"You haven't upset me!"

His hands were tight on the steering wheel, his features set.

Claire wished she hadn't said anything.

The sporty little car glided past mile after mile of the same dry rocky ranch land that she had passed yesterday, more slowly, in her car. The same patches of low scrub, spread out from the two-lane blacktop county road, and in the distance rose pyramid-shaped hills and the jagged tips of mountains.

When the first signs of a town appeared, Tanner finally broke into speech once more, his subject unchanged. "I truly do love this car," he said tightly. "It's just— I had a good friend who wanted one, too. And he didn't get his."

Claire glanced at him. Had he thought of nothing else all the while he'd been driving? "Why not?" she asked. "The cost?"

His answer was stark. "He died."

She frowned. "What of?"

"A heart attack."

"How old was he?"

"My age. Thirty-six."

Her frown deepened. "That's very young for a heart attack." When he said nothing, she inquired further, "Was it unexpected? Did he have a history of heart trouble?"

"Very…and no, he didn't have a history."

"I'm sorry." Claire's simple condolence hung in the air between them.

Traffic increased as they neared the center of town, necessitating Tanner's concentration. Moments later—in an apparent effort to free himself of his preoccupation—he exclaimed, "Hey! The place is still here! That store over there—" He pointed to a row of brick-faced buildings where the parking in front was set at an angle. "That's where Rafe bought me my first pair of boots."

Claire gazed at the old-fashioned stores. To visit Del Norte was to step back in time about fifty years. A hardware store was located next to a saddlery. An ice cream parlor abutted a five-and-dime store. A family-owned drugstore was next to a local grocery store. The town catered to the needs of the surrounding ranches, bringing them civilization. But civilization on *their* terms.

"We'll look there for my boots," Tanner said. "They sell other gear, too. First, though, I'll give you the tour."

"I'm sure I could find my way if I ever needed to. The town's not very large."

He shook his head. "Mae said to show you around, so that's what I'm going to do. Believe me, I don't need *more* trouble." The charm in his smile completely eclipsed his earlier sadness. "Rafe runs the ranch, Mae runs the family—but overall, she's still the boss."

"Are you afraid of her?" Claire asked curiously.

"Anyone who can intimidate Rafe can intimidate me. And he's the Parker most like her."

They drove past more quaint buildings and businesses. Past homes and a car dealership, a motel and a tavern called the Watering Hole. Then Tanner turned back to the center of town, where he pointed out the sheriff's office and the jail. The new jail, he said, had been built since his last visit to the area.

"Axel told me Jodie Parker's husband is the sheriff," Claire commented.

"Tate Connelly, yeah. I've heard he's had a hard time over the past couple of years. Got shot up pretty bad doing some kind of special task force work for the state. Almost died. Took him a long time to recover."

Claire remembered a previous client who'd had a freak accident while getting out of his neighbor's pickup. His hunting rifle had discharged, almost killing him, but he'd eventually recovered. "Bullets can do a lot of damage."

He looked at her, his brown eyes serious. "Have you ever nursed someone through something like that?"

"Once."

"Do you nurse mostly old people?"

"Mostly." Claire pointed out the window at a complex they were about to pass and asked quickly, "Is that a hospital?"

The one-story structure set a short distance from the highway had all the elements of a hospital, but without a sign.

"Del Norte General Hospital," Tanner confirmed.

Claire's attention fixed on a pair of office suites off to one side of the common parking area. Doctors' offices? She doubted that such a small town could boast more than two or three.

"Do we have time to stop?" she asked as an idea suddenly hit her.

"Sure," Tanner replied, but he didn't sound enthusiastic. He turned the sports car off the road.

Claire searched her memory for the name Shannon had mentioned. *Dr. Stevens.* That was it.

When Tanner accelerated toward the hospital, Claire said, "No, over there," and pointed to the offices. "If he has a moment, I'd like to introduce myself to Miss Parker's doctor." Once the car rolled to a stop, she said, "I won't be long," and got out.

The brass plate on the first door read Carl Stevens, M.D., General Practice. Claire was in and out of the office in seconds.

"The receptionist said he's at the emergency room. That I should go there."

Tanner had been staring across the parking lot at the rather nondescript emergency room entrance. He said quietly, "I'll come with you."

"There's no need."

"I want to," he assured her, and unfolded his length from the car.

Their entry into the emergency room drew the attention of a uniformed nurse posted at the workstation. Her gaze swept professionally over them.

"The main entrance to the hospital is over there," she said, pointing.

"We're looking for Dr. Stevens," Claire said. "His office sent us."

"He's with a patient now." The standard reply was promptly negated when a pleasant-faced man with dark hair and a knee-length white jacket came out of a treatment room at the end of the short hall. Two adults and a little boy of about five trailed behind him. The boy snuffled as he supported his bandaged arm.

"He'll be fine," the doctor told the parents. "The swelling should be down in a couple of hours, and in a few days he won't even notice the scratches. Next time, Billy, don't put your hand down a pipe because you want to see what's in the bottom."

"Oh, he won't!" the woman assured him firmly. "You've learned your lesson, haven't you, Billy?"

The little boy nodded solemnly as his father clasped the doctor's hand.

The doctor's gaze then moved to Claire and Tanner, and they were once again subjected to a professional assessment.

Claire quickly introduced herself. "I'm Claire Hannaford, Dr. Stevens. I've just arrived to care for Mae Parker. I was told that you're her physician?"

The man folded his arms. "So she finally took my advice."

"And this—" Claire turned to introduce Tanner, but he'd moved to the open doorway of the nearest empty treatment room and stood there, as if mesmerized. For a moment she was unsure whether to complete the introduction. She had no idea if the two men already knew each other. Still, she forged on. "And this is Tanner Reid. You, uh, advised Miss Parker to hire home assistance?"

"A couple of months ago," the doctor said. "But she wouldn't consider it then."

"She never said."

Dr. Stevens laughed shortly. "There's a lot she never says." His gaze narrowed. "You're with the Smithfield agency out of Midland?"

"Yes."

"I assured her your agency was excellent. When did you arrive?"

"Yesterday evening." Claire glanced back at Tanner. He still hadn't moved. She frowned.

The doctor checked his watch. "I wish I had more time, but with only two physicians, things sometimes get a little rushed."

Claire apologized quickly. "I just wanted to introduce myself, let you know that I'm at the ranch. I didn't mean to keep you."

"You haven't," the doctor said. "We really do

need to talk—'' He stopped and also looked at Tanner. ''Is your friend all right?''

Claire walked to Tanner's side and touched his arm. The gentle contact caused him to start. When his gaze flew to hers, it was filled with horror.

''Tanner?'' she murmured.

Then she understood. He'd just told her about his friend's untimely death. If he'd been with the man when he was stricken and accompanied him to the hospital, putting himself in another emergency room could trigger any number of terrible memories.

He stared blankly at her, still not released from his horror.

To stave off embarrassment for him, Claire slipped her arm through his and gave a mild tug. ''We have to go, Tanner. Dr. Stevens has an appointment.''

''Are you sure?'' the doctor asked, frowning as he stepped closer.

''Sure, yeah, gotta go.'' Tanner sounded like a robot firing back a series of responses.

Claire smiled tightly at the doctor and drew Tanner through the exit. She could feel the doctor and nurse watching them all the way.

Once outside, she asked, ''Are you all right?''

He nodded. He was still pale, still tense, but he was better.

''Why didn't you tell me you might have difficulty?'' she demanded as they started across the parking lot. ''How long has it been since your friend died?''

''I had to do it,'' he said quietly. ''I had to face it.'' He spoke the words aloud, but mostly to himself.

''But maybe not this soon,'' Claire murmured. ''How long has it been?'' she repeated.

''Three weeks,'' he choked.

''And you were with him while the doctors—''

Tanner laughed, but without amusement. ''Yeah.''

Just as she'd suspected. ''That's a very difficult thing to watch.''

At the car, he pulled his arm free of hers, rolled his shoulders and jerked his head to one side. Then he saw her into the passenger seat and slid behind the wheel. But instead of starting the engine, he apologized.

''I'm sorry to zone out on you like that,'' he said huskily. ''I didn't expect— I hope I didn't embarrass you too much.''

''I don't get embarrassed at something like that,'' Claire answered in all honesty.

He looked at her for several long seconds, then said softly, ''Thanks.''

CHAPTER FIVE

TANNER EASED THE SPORTS car into the garage and parked it in the same slot they'd vacated earlier. LeRoy was nowhere to be seen. "Back with a half hour to spare," he said easily, turning to Claire. "Plenty of time for the tour here."

Since leaving the hospital he'd tried to make up for his mental lapse. He wanted her to enjoy the trip, not just tolerate it—and him—as she'd done at first. She'd smiled as he joked with the clerk in the saddlery, and appreciated the ice cream cone he'd bought each of them as they strolled along the sidewalk. But she still held herself apart.

He'd behaved like such an idiot in the emergency room. Yet she hadn't condemned or disapproved...or, as she claimed, been embarrassed.

"Surely I've seen enough," she replied. "I saw the corrals as we drove by, and I know where the garage and barn are."

"It won't take long," he assured her. "And Mae will ask."

He stepped out of the car, his feet snug in his new boots, and retrieved the shopping bag from the trunk. If he was to stay on the ranch and learn the work, he wanted his own gear. He'd bought enough jeans and shirts not to have to go on borrowing from Rafe.

Claire fell into step beside him as they exited the garage.

"That's the cook house," he said, indicating the add-on structure directly ahead of them. "The bunkhouse opens off it around the front. That's where most of the single cowboys live." He led her to the opposite side, to an open space surrounded by a group of weathered buildings. Each was long and low, with a roof that extended to form a narrow front porch.

"The bunkhouse—" He motioned to the structure he'd mentioned earlier, then swept a finger in a wide circle, ticking off the others. "The ranch office, the tack room and storerooms, the workshop."

He took her into the ranch office as Mae had directed, and smiled as her eyes widened. Her surprise echoed his when he'd first realized that such a large operation had such a simple heart. The room was bare except for a desk, a chair, a large metal file cabinet and a yellowed painting of a Hereford bull that hung on the far wall.

Tanner was about to comment on the lack of creature comforts when Rafe strode onto the narrow porch. After swatting dust from his clothes, he stepped into the room. The instant he saw them he pulled up short.

"Hey, Rafe," Tanner said, greeting him sociably. "Just showing Claire around. Mae wants her to know where everything is."

"You don't say," Rafe returned evenly, then dropped into the swivel chair. "LeRoy tells me you've been to town."

Tanner nodded. "Brought Claire along, too."

"What'd you think of it?" Rafe's dark eyes moved to her.

"It's...very nice," Claire responded. "Small."

"Not what you're used to, huh?"

"I've worked in small towns before."

"Ever work on a ranch?"

"Not like this one."

Rafe held her gaze; hers never wavered.

At last he said, "Shannon's sent word for you to come over to our place. She doesn't think you got a good enough welcome yesterday."

Easily discernible was Rafe's differing opinion. Tanner shifted uncomfortably.

Claire repeated what she'd said earlier. "I'm not here to socialize, Mr. Parker."

"You're not here to go on tours, either," Rafe

snapped, his veneer of civility wearing thin, ''but here you are.''

Tanner intervened. ''It was at Mae's instruction, Rafe. Claire didn't want to do it.''

''Then she should've refused.''

Before Tanner could speak again, Claire answered for herself. ''From what I've seen so far, the Parkers aren't easy to say 'no' to. Particularly Miss Parker.''

Tanner took Claire's arm. She'd helped him at the hospital; he'd help her here. She didn't seem to understand just how difficult Rafe could make her life outside the main house. ''We'll leave you to it, then,'' he said, and shepherded her to the door.

''Don't forget, Miss Hannaford,'' Rafe called after them. ''Shannon's expectin' you. Sometime today would be good.''

Claire turned to ask calmly, ''Is that an order?''

''It's a request,'' Rafe barked.

After pulling her outside, Tanner headed for the path, where he urged her toward the compound.

''Is the tour over?'' she asked levelly.

''You saw the pens and corrals when we drove by, you said. You've had enough, haven't you?''

''Actually, I've had more than enough.''

The underlying pithiness of her reply gave Tanner a glimpse into her true feelings. The sparring match with Rafe had unsettled her more than she'd likely admit.

He pulled up and faced her. If he could get her to understand—

"You realize what's going on here, don't you?" he said seriously. "Your arrival hit them in a way they don't know how to deal with. Mae's always been this amazing force in their lives. She's the same generation as Rafe and LeRoy's grandfather. The oldest living Parker. She didn't stop riding horses until she was eighty, and then only because she broke her leg. She managed the ranch after Rafe's father died, then turned it over years later when Rafe was ready. They butted heads—they still do! It's hard for the family to watch her get older, get weaker." He paused. "That's where you come in. To them, you're the symbol she's not invincible."

"No one is invincible," Claire said. "Not where death is concerned. We all—"

Tanner's thoughts jumped to Danny. The way the two of them had been laughing about something at the office, then moments later Danny had collapsed in terrible pain, pale and weak and gasping for breath.

A muscle ticked in his jaw.

She must have seen it and realized the connection, because she immediately apologized. "I'm sorry. I didn't mean— Your friend—"

"No, you're right," Tanner said flatly. "It happens."

He'd tried to help. He'd yelled for his assistant to call 911, then administered every emergency procedure that he knew.

"You were very close," she stated softly.

"We'd had a business together."

"Had?" She seized on the word. To keep him talking? To keep him from completely zoning out as he had earlier at the hospital?

"We'd just sold it," he divulged. "Signed the papers the day before. A dream come true. Then—" He stopped and drew a breath, trying not to let bitter irony overwhelm him.

On the way to the hospital he'd called Danny's wife to tell her that her husband had been stricken. Later, he'd had to break the news when she arrived that Danny had lost his fight for life. Then he'd endured what followed...when Elaine slammed into him in anguished condemnation, blaming *him* for everything that had happened.

"It's not your fault," Claire said quietly, interrupting his painful thoughts.

Tanner's body jerked.

How did she know? He'd told no one what Elaine had said to him.

He played for time, trying to decide how to react. He shifted the shopping bag from hand to hand, rubbed the back of his neck, checked his watch.

In the end he pretended she'd said nothing.

"Mae will be pleased we're back early," he said heartily. "Tell her—tell her I won't be in for lunch. That I've…forgotten something. I'll, uh, see you later." Then he escaped, striding purposefully back down the path toward the work area. Inside himself, though, he was shaken—as shaken as the Parkers had been the day before by the latest addition to the ranch.

"YOU'RE BACK!" MAE PARKER declared, looking up at Claire from the numerous papers that littered her rosewood desk. The black cane hung suspended by its handle near her right hand. "Did you enjoy yourself?"

"Surprisingly, yes. I did."

"Why 'surprisingly'?" she demanded, her eyes narrowing.

"Because I didn't want to go."

"What'd you think of Del Norte?"

Claire gave her almost the same answer as she'd given Rafe. "It's small, but interesting. We had an ice cream cone."

Mae's lips twitched. "Tanner really put himself out."

"He did, actually," Claire said.

Mae subjected her to another probing look. "What else happened?" she demanded.

The woman was gifted at divining secrets, but Claire was equally adept at protecting confidences. She shifted subjects adroitly. "I met your doctor, Dr. Stevens."

"I didn't mean for you to do that!"

"He seemed relieved to know I'm here."

"Oh, he did, did he?" The older woman lifted her chin.

"He told me he advised you months ago to get help."

"Doctors!" Mae bristled. "Always givin' advice. Most times about things a person can well do without!"

"There are times, though, when you can't," Claire contradicted quietly.

"Didn't I call your agency? Didn't I hire you? Doctors!" the woman repeated in disgust.

Claire wondered what additional advice the physician had given her—advice that must have been unsettling.

Mae tried to stand up but had difficulty doing it. Claire reached to help her. Once the matriarch got to her feet, though, additional assistance was brushed away.

"I've got somethin' for you," the woman said, crossing the room. "Best thing I know to teach you about this place. While you're here, you might as well learn what you can." She extracted a modest volume from the nearest bookcase. "Here," she said. "It's the Parker family history. Shannon helped me put it together some years back. I wanted each and every Parker to see their heritage in print, particularly the ones that live off the ranch."

"There are more Parkers?" Claire asked as she accepted the book.

"Quite a few. Most are scattered across the state, but a couple live outside it."

Claire examined the volume. A family's heritage. Page after page of the people who'd come before them. She smoothed the fine leather cover...and didn't realize that her deep sense of awe was written on her face.

"What is it?" Mae demanded. "Why are you lookin' at it like that?"

"I'm...impressed," Claire hedged, telling the truth at the same time trying to cover her slip. She flipped through a few pages. "I'll definitely read it."

"Do that," Mae snapped. "Then give it back. There're only a couple of copies left."

"Oh, I will," Claire assured her.

Mae glanced at the clock on a shelf. "Marie'll be ready to serve lunch. Tanner come in with you?"

"He asked me to tell you he'll be in later. He forgot something."

"Then it'll just be us," Mae said, and started for the door. "By the way," she added over her shoulder, "you'll find Marie a lot more on the friendly side. She and I had a good long talk, and she's given me her word that she won't take her bruised feelin's out on you anymore."

Claire nodded, but thought it prudent to reserve judgment.

RAFE'S LOW CHUCKLE SHOOK Tanner from his abstraction.

"I'm sorry, I didn't hear what you said," he apologized.

Smiling, Rafe shook his head. "You haven't been hearin' much of anythin' since you got back. What happened out there? You and that little nurse have a set-to?"

"No," Tanner denied quickly. "We just— I—"

"Maybe I should put it another way. 'Set-to'

might be too strong a term. How about 'exchange'?''

Tanner had taken a seat on the corner of the desk after returning to the ranch office. He abandoned it to stand in the open doorway. He'd told no one here about what had happened to Danny. Or what had followed at the hospital. He'd hardly been able to *think* about it. And for Claire to have seen so easily inside him—

"She's not exactly the shrinkin' violet she first shows up as," Rafe observed. "What'd you find out about her? Anything we should know about?"

"Why? Do you think she's an escaped ax murderer?" Tanner asked sardonically.

"Nah," Rafe quipped. "Not big enough."

Tanner made himself smile as he shrugged. "She seems okay to me. Nice enough. Doesn't say a lot."

"Which looks to suit Mae just fine," Rafe muttered.

"Then maybe that should be good enough. If Mae likes her…"

"I just wish she'da let us in on it. Not pulled a nurse out of her hat like she was some kinda magician!"

"Mom's called her a magician before, too." Tanner laughed. "Like in the way she always seems to know things."

"Aunt Mae rarely got the jump on Mom. Used to drive her crazy that she couldn't. My daddy never let things go too far, though. When Mae got spittin' mad about something, he'd step in and tell her to forget it. Then he'd tell Mom to just let it go. And they'd rub on together. Maybe if I'd been older when Mom met your dad, I could've done the same. Saved us all a lot of upset."

"Mom's happy where she is."

"I know. She wouldn't change a thing. She's enjoyed helpin' raise you kids."

Tanner broached a tender subject. Something he'd been thinking about since the night before. "Do you think we should call Mom and tell her to come for a visit? Before Mae—"

Rafe shot him a hard look. "There's plenty of time left for visits."

"But what if there's not?" Tanner persisted. Danny had had no idea how short his time was.

"I *won't* rush things," Rafe growled.

Tanner inhaled sharply. He needed to block these thoughts of Danny. "What do you want me to do around here if I'm not going to work on the records?" he asked.

The edge left Rafe's voice, to be replaced by calculation. "Ah...but you *are* goin' to work on the records. At least, a few of 'em. So we can show Mae what we're talkin' about. Like I said, she used to be dead set against usin' a telephone, too, but over these past few years when she's stayed closer to home, she's sure kept the phone lines burnin'. Only, we won't let her know what you're doin' for a while. To keep her from havin' a hissy fit. Rest of the time, when you're not workin' here, you can do what she said and learn about ranchin'. That is, if you want to.''

''Sure,'' Tanner agreed. He glanced around the no-frills office. ''What about a computer?''

''Shannon has the one she uses for her family histories at our place. We can move it out here for a while. She says she doesn't mind.''

The vaunted Parker family history was something Tanner had heard about. Several neighbors had asked Shannon to compile theirs, as well.

''It's a few years old, isn't it?'' he asked diplomatically.

''About ten,'' Rafe said.

Tanner couldn't hide his appalled reaction, which caused Rafe to smile.

''A little too old, huh?'' he asked.

''Like the difference between a Model T and an Indie racer!''

''Well, write down what you need and I'll get it. Could take a few days, though. We don't want Mae noticin'.''

Tanner nodded in complete agreement.

WHEN MARIE SERVED LUNCH, she made every effort to be cordial to Claire.

For her part, Claire determined to finish the entire bowl of thick vegetable soup, even though she wasn't the least bit hungry.

Mae finished her bowl with gusto, just as she did the thick slice of homemade brown bread that accompanied it. Then she sat back and said, "We usually have lunch around noon. I made an exception today so you could have your look around. Most days, it'll just be you and Tanner in here. Marie brings my meal to the office."

"I thought Tanner was Rafe's guest."

"He is. But Rafe and Shannon are runnin' out of room at their place. They have three kids and nowhere to put him. I have two empty bedrooms upstairs, so he's stayin' here. Which reminds me, I want to talk to you about that extra room."

Marie appeared from the kitchen to collect their used dishes. Mae, temporarily derailed, complimented her effort. "Excellent as always, Marie. I'm surprised Jodie hasn't already come rushin' out."

"I've put some away for her like I always do, just in case," the housekeeper replied, looking pleased. She disappeared but returned seconds later with a platter of fresh fruit.

Mae chose two sugar-glazed strawberries and a cinnamon apple slice as she reverted to her earlier topic. "About that extra room. You need a place to use in your spare time, where you can be on your own. I'd say you could sleep there, too, but—" she frowned "—it's too far away if I was to need you in the night. That's why...the parlor."

Claire tried to ease the awkward moment. "I prefer to sleep near my charges. Upstairs would be difficult."

Mae fired a look that checked the veracity of her statement. Then she asked, "Did Tanner tell you anything about himself? About why he's here? About his family?"

"I heard the disagreement about the ranch records."

"Rafe's determined to do somethin' he shouldn't and he's brought Tanner here to see it done. I can't understand why the boy's in such a hurry! We've been usin' the same method for keepin' our records for as long as I can remember. Computers lose things. Eat 'em up. Blip...and they're gone. Or so I've heard. I keep *tellin'* him, but he won't listen!"

"I don't know anything about computers," Claire said.

"Well, Tanner does." Mae stabbed a strawberry with her fork. "He ran some kind of software company out in California. That's the stuff that makes a computer work, isn't it?''

"Miss Parker, I—''

Mae glanced at her irritably. ''Call me Mae. My name's really Mary Louise, but no one's called me that since I learned to talk.''

"I'd rather call you Miss Parker.'' It was important to Claire not to cross the line between service and friendship. More than important, it was imperative.

"And *I'd* rather you called me Mae. 'Miss Parker' makes me feel all schoolmarmish.'' She went back to her story about Tanner, as if there'd been no interruption. ''He's just sold his company for a lot of money. You'd think he'd be over the moon. But he's not. Young people.'' She shook her head. ''Takes more and more energy to figure 'em out these days. Then, again, I don't know Tanner all that well. Did he tell you how his daddy came to marry Rafe's mama? How she went against what I told her? What I *plainly* told her?''

"No, ma'am.''

"What'd the two of you talk about, then?'' Mae demanded.

"He showed me the town and ranch headquarters, just as you said.''

Mae dropped her fork, the berry still attached, and heaved a sigh. ''Well, we'll have to get into

this another time. Right now, I'm gonna take me
a nap. It's been a *hard* couple of days.''

Claire watched as the woman made a point of
getting up and crossing the room on her own
power.

The show of independence made her wonder if
she was expected *not* to follow. Despite the lack
of instruction, she caught up with the woman in
the hall and Mae made no objection.

An instruction was handed out, however, once
the matriarch was in bed.

''Go take a look at that upstairs room. See if
there's anything Axel can do to make it nice for
you. It's the second room down the hall. Then
wake me in an hour, will you?''

On her way out of the bedroom suite, Claire set
the volume of the Parker family history on the table near her single bed. She had mixed feelings
about reading it. She wanted to, then again she
didn't. All those people who'd come before...

She saw no one as she moved into the entryway,
then mounted the stairs to the second floor.

The second room down the hall, Mae had said.
Which meant the first room was Tanner's. The
door was closed, so she had no idea if he was
inside or not.

When she opened the second door, she found a
spacious room decorated in the same Spanish fla-

vor as the other public rooms of the house. Heavy
dark furniture, stark white walls, a bright woven
rug between twin beds and one placed before a pair
of French doors that opened onto a balcony.

Claire's gaze locked on the French doors and the
balcony. She moved across the room as if drawn,
heading straight for the black wrought-iron railing.

She closed her eyes. A private place of her own!
A hideaway where she could be free to dream and
think. She'd only ever experienced such luxury on
vacation—those infrequent bright spots she allowed herself between patients.

She drew a breath of sun-heated air…and someone called her name.

Her eyes opened and she focused on the hard-
packed gravel drive below, where Shannon stood,
her wheat-colored hair gleaming brightly in the
sunlight.

"I was just coming to see you," Shannon said.
"To invite you over for coffee. Rafe was supposed
to ask, but—" She smiled wryly. "I know how
off-putting he can be sometimes. Has he talked to
you?"

"Yes," Claire replied.

"If you have some free time, there are a couple
of people at my place who'd really like to meet
you."

"Miss Parker's resting. I can come," Claire returned. What else could she say? Her presence on the balcony spoke for itself.

Shannon beamed. "Good!"

"But I can't stay long," Claire added, giving herself an out. "I'll have to wake Miss Parker."

"Do you know which is our house?" Shannon asked, and pointed to the nearest structure on the left arm of the drive. "That's ours. Harriet and LeRoy live over there." She indicated the house farthest away on the right. "The one closer to you on that side belongs to Darlene and Thomas. They're Rafe and LeRoy's aunt and uncle. They're off on a Scandinavian holiday right now. Gib and Thomas are brothers…you haven't met Gib yet, have you? He lives in the house next door to ours." She laughed ruefully and shook her head. "Here I am, trying to make up for our rudeness yesterday, and I'm reeling off names and relationships. And I know better! Overwhelmed isn't quite a strong enough word, is it?"

Claire made herself smile. She was going to have to enforce a professional relationship with these people. They seemed to want to gather her in, while she, most definitely, wanted to remain apart.

"Is five minutes all right with you?" Shannon checked. When Claire nodded, she waved and set off for her house.

Once again Claire closed her eyes and tried to regain the earlier magic. But it was gone. She sighed. Maybe it would be best to get all the introductions over with. See everything she was supposed to see, talk to everyone she needed to talk to. Then she'd be done with it and she could concentrate on her job.

"I thought I heard voices," Tanner remarked from nearby.

He stood in the open doorway of his bedroom, framed by a set of French doors that matched those behind her. Claire hadn't realized the two rooms shared the same balcony.

"I'm going to Shannon's house," she stated defensively, momentarily caught off guard.

"So I heard."

His brown eyes were hooded, his expression unrevealing.

Did he regret having told her about his friend?

"Miss Parker is allowing me to use this room. In the daytime," she hastily amended, then realized how silly it sounded.

His lips pulled into a smile. "I don't snore."

"It's not that," she returned quickly. Again, a little *too* quickly.

He looked particularly good standing there—a fact Claire couldn't help but notice. The only thing was, she didn't *want* to notice it.

"I know," he said. "Mae needs you near her at night."

"Exactly," she agreed.

The heightened feelings of unreality Claire had dealt with for most of the day had increased over the past few moments. Shaking them away, she sent him a tight, polite little smile and hurried back into the bedroom.

It seemed she had another issue to enforce!

CHAPTER SIX

SHANNON WELCOMED CLAIRE into her modest home, then escorted her into the living room, where two women Claire had never seen before were ensconced on a sofa and chair.

One was about Claire's age, willowy, with bright copper-colored hair, elfin features and golden-brown eyes. The other, a few years older, had chestnut hair and similar eyes. Both returned her look intently.

Shannon smiled. "More introductions, I'm afraid, Claire. This is Jodie." She indicated the redhead. "Jodie is Gib's daughter. She's married to Tate Connelly, the Briggs County sheriff. They live in Del Norte. And on the sofa is Christine. Christine's husband is the ranch foreman, Morgan Hughes. They live in Little Springs—that's one of the ranch divisions not far from here. Christine's a blood Parker, too."

"It's very nice to meet you," Claire said.

Harriet entered the room from the rear of the

house, carrying a beaker of freshly brewed coffee. She, too, greeted Claire warmly. "Glad you could make it," she said, and placed the pot on a trivet next to a set of cups and saucers arranged on a low table.

"Claire's come to us through an agency in Midland," Shannon said, indicating Claire should take a seat before she and Harriet took theirs.

"Midland," Christine repeated, watching Claire settle on a chair cushion. "I hadn't expected you to be from so far away."

"How did Aunt Mae find you?" Jodie demanded sharply, leaning forward.

Claire met the redhead's inhospitable gaze. The others might be willing to play nice, but Jodie wasn't. Which confirmed what Claire had half expected—that this wasn't so much an invitation for coffee as an opportunity to question her.

"Through her doctor," she replied levelly. "He told me he—"

Christine turned to Shannon. "Didn't you say she hadn't talked to Dr. Stevens yet?"

"That's what you told us yesterday," Harriet asserted, her eyes narrowing suspiciously on Claire.

"I met him when I went into Del Norte this morning with Tanner. Miss Parker insisted that he take me along when he went to town."

"So, that's what LeRoy was goin' on about!" Harriet declared, all at once enlightened. "He told me you and Tanner had gone off together. But I didn't—"

"What did Dr. Stevens say?" Jodie cut in, reverting to the pertinent facts.

Claire met her gaze. "That he was familiar with my agency and had recommended it to her."

"I *mean* about Aunt Mae."

"We didn't have time to talk. He was on duty in the emergency room."

Jodie groaned her frustration.

"Don't borrow trouble, Jodie," Shannon advised quickly.

Jodie reeled off facts. "Aunt Mae passes out on us...*twice*. Then we find out she's done it more often than that. She hires herself a nurse. I don't know how the rest of you can sit here and not be worried, too."

"We *are* worried," Harriet countered earnestly.

Shannon reached along the sofa for Jodie's hand. "I told you when I called that we—" She glanced ruefully at Claire, aware that her words had removed any doubt that this was an unplanned meeting. She continued firmly, "We *are* worried, Jodie, just as Harriet says. But what can we do? We can't force Mae to do something she doesn't want to do."

"She should have tests!" Jodie burst out tightly. "See what's going on! See if it's anything the doctors can fix. Maybe she needs a pacemaker. A test would tell us that, wouldn't it?"

Harriet shook her head sadly, "She won't listen to us, Jodie. Not about that. You know what it was like tryin' to make Tate listen to what was good for him. And Mae's ten times worse!"

Claire had forgotten what Tanner had said about Tate Connelly's long and difficult recovery from bullet wounds received in the line of duty. She looked at Jodie with more interest.

"We can't just do *nothing*," Jodie exclaimed, a single tear rolling down her cheek.

Her naked fear fed the others' disquiet.

"If you were to learn that Mae needed tests and was refusing them, would you tell us?" Christine asked Claire.

"If she needed tests, I'd urge her to have them." Claire eluded a direct reply.

"That's not what I asked," Christine retorted. "Would you tell us?"

Yesterday Claire had assumed the family knew about Mae Parker's multiple "spells." She didn't want to make another mistake. Diplomatically, she asked, "Don't any of you feel comfortable enough with her doctor to talk with him yourself?"

"We didn't know there was a recurring problem...until you arrived."

Claire's gaze traveled from Christine to Shannon and Harriet. "As I tried to explain yesterday, it's not unusual for someone her age to—"

"You don't understand!" Jodie broke in. "That's *not* Aunt Mae!"

"Jodie—" Shannon squeezed the young woman's hand.

Harriet twisted her interlocked fingers. Christine stared at the floor.

Claire waited in silence, letting the family members compose themselves. People all too often had a way of not wanting to see what was in front of them, of not wanting to admit what they already knew.

Shannon cleared her throat, then said quietly, "We asked you here to apologize for the way we behaved yesterday. It's not your fault Mae sent us six-ways-for-Sunday by hiring you without telling us, or that we're *still* six-ways-for-Sunday because she felt the need to hire you at all. We're just...concerned for her. That's all."

"I understand," Claire said.

She did her best to project an aura of calm, which seemed to work, if only briefly. The tension among the women began to lessen.

Finally, Harriet said, ''We had no idea what Mae was planning.''

''She didn't tell us anything,'' Jodie confirmed.

''Just...watch out for her for us, will you?'' Christine murmured. ''Let us know if there's any way...anything we can do.''

''I will,'' Claire said. She checked her watch. Barely twenty minutes had passed since she'd first entered the house, and the coffee had been completely forgotten. Yet this was the proper moment for her to leave. The family needed to be on their own, free of the person whose presence so disturbed them.

She stood up. ''I should go back. Miss Parker—''

''Of course,'' Shannon agreed, and rose smoothly to accompany her to the door.

Claire started to follow her out of the room when a strikingly realistic oil painting caught her attention. It was a ranch scene in which a long lean cowboy had just placed a saddle on the back of a young horse. The horse's legs were stiff, his head twisted back, his whole body resisting the unaccustomed weight. The man looked to be talking to him, calming him, gaining his trust before he took the next step of securing the cinch.

Shannon stopped and let her gaze follow

Claire's. She smiled as she asked, "Does the cow-boy look familiar?"

After studying the man in more detail, Claire saw, to her surprise, that it was Rafe Parker.

"That's Gib's work," Shannon said. "Jodie's dad. He's come to be a fairly well-known western artist. There's more of a demand for his paintings than he's willing to sell." She reached into a book-shelf. "And this is Harriet's handiwork. It's just been published. She wrote the story and Gib did the illustrations."

She handed Claire a children's book. On the cover an appealing baby coyote sat beside a blooming yucca cactus in an open area very similar to the Parker Ranch. The name Harriet Dunn was imprinted beneath the title, *Chico the Cheerful Coyote,* and at the bottom was the notation, Illus-trations by Gibson Parker.

"Look inside," Shannon urged. "The kids all love it. Even Ward, our oldest. He's eight and a half and pretends he's too old for such things, but he cozies up next to us when I read it to Nate and Nikki, our younger two. I've even caught him try-ing to draw Chico. He's pretty good at it, actu-ally."

Claire leafed through the pages, impressed.

"*Chico* is really Harriet's second book," Shan-non continued as she reached for a thicker volume.

"This was her first. It's for older kids." She showed the book to Claire then put it back. "Have you seen the painting of ranch headquarters in Mae's living room? Mae asked Gib to paint it for her ninetieth birthday…which was something, because for years Gib had to keep his artwork a secret since Mae wouldn't approve. Now he has a studio of his own and spends as much time as he wants there. He doesn't mind interruptions, by the way, if you'd like to see it."

Although the invitation was tempting, since Claire dabbled in drawing herself, it was another diversion she didn't need. She shook her head.

"Gib loves to have people drop by, doesn't he, Jodie?" Shannon prompted.

Jodie nodded unenthusiastically.

Claire and Shannon moved to the front door.

"I still don't feel we've treated you properly," Shannon said as Claire stepped outside. "In normal times we're not nearly so ungracious to visitors. I know—we'll just have to do this again, and next time without the third degree so we can actually drink our coffee!"

Claire returned the woman's smile, but made no commitment.

MAE AWAKENED, WITHOUT prompting, before the end of the allotted hour and came into the parlor to surprise Claire, who was absorbed in the Parker family history.

She hadn't gone very far in the book, but she'd already read about the founders of the Parker Ranch—the two brothers who'd arrived in West Texas in the early 1850s and claimed a section of land. Through hard work and determination, they had survived bandit and Indian raids and a serious scarcity of water. By the time of the Civil War, they were settled enough to supply cattle to the Confederacy. Instead of pocketing the money, as some of their peers did, they increased the size of their herd, buying a dozen longhorns for each one they sold. When the Confederacy eventually fell and the currency became worthless, Parker money was safely on the hoof.

Other states were carved or born. Texas was made of hoof and horn. A photograph of a cross-stitch sampler with that adage had been included in the book. The text beneath credited Martha Parker with the stitchery.

Claire had been examining the photo when Mae reached over her shoulder and tapped the page.

"I have the original of that if you want to see it," Mae said.

Startled by the woman's unexpected appearance, Claire forgot her determined resolve to remain emotionally detached from the Parker family.

"Oh! Yes, that would be—" she quickly muted her enthusiasm "—very interesting."

Mae lifted an eyebrow but didn't comment. "I'll show it to you the next time we're in my office." She tested the bed's narrow mattress with her hand. "You're sure this thing's comfortable enough to sleep on?"

"Perfectly."

"What about that bedroom upstairs? You want Axel to shift anything around for you?"

"It's perfectly fine as well," Claire said.

Mae looked around the room. "You must feel like a fish in a glass bowl out here." She turned her observation on Claire. "You're a pretty little thing. Seem intelligent. Why'd you pick this line of work? Can't be fun traveling from one place to another to take care of people."

"I'm used to it," Claire said simply.

Obviously Mae wasn't satisfied with her answer. "A cowboy gets used to steppin' in cow dung, too, but that don't mean he enjoys it!"

Claire's lips twitched. "I'm not a cowboy."

"You gonna answer me or not?" Mae demanded.

"I do it...because it's what I do."

"Didn't you ever want to be one of those fancy high-powered women executives we hear so much about these days, with their big offices and their big titles? What about a family? Do you want one a' those?''

"I don't expect it, no," Claire answered levelly, her fingers tightening on the history book.

"Why not?"

"Miss Parker—"

"Call me *Mae*. This family is the center of my life, and if you consider that old-fashioned or not worth a hill of beans, I want to know about it now! There's some things that need doin' I told you about, remember? And—" she paused, only to finish fiercely "—and I want to hear what you have to say!"

Claire never talked about herself with a patient. Never talked about herself with anyone. In this instance, though, her usual reticence would only cause more problems. She took a breath and answered carefully, "Of course I think you loving your family is important. I've been reading about Virgil and Gibson. About the way they started the ranch and all they had to endure. They did it for the Parkers who came after them. That's highly admirable. So is the way your family pulls together today."

Mae seemed to like what she heard. "I had a politician tell me once that we Parkers are like yaks. When we scent danger, we put our backsides in a circle and face out, ready to take on whatever comes. To this day, I'm not completely sure if he meant it as a compliment. That man, by the way, was Shannon's daddy, Nathan Bradley. The two of us used to have some pretty good arguments. Most of which I won.''

Claire seized upon the shift in subject. ''Shannon's father was a politician?''

''He sure was. One of the better ones. Actually had a conscience.'' Mae became lost in memory for a moment. Then she asked, ''You still want to see that piece of stitchery? My Mama made it for my daddy.''

''Your mother was Martha Parker?'' Claire asked. The allure of such a long family line tugged at her. What must it be like to know who you were and to be able to read about the people who preceded you?

Mae nodded. ''She married Watt Parker, one of Gibson's sons. They had me, my brother Jeff—Jeff was Rafe, Jodie and LeRoy's granddaddy—and our older brother, Theodore.'' She stopped to give Claire a beady look. ''Don't think I'm not onto what you've just done, young lady. You never did tell me how you got into nursing…or anythin' else about yourself. But it's early days yet. I'll get it outta you.''

The matriarch motioned for Claire to follow her to her office. Once there, she directed her to remove a cardboard box from a closed area beneath one of the bookshelves. Claire placed the box on the low table in front of the dark green leather couch.

It turned out to be a treasure trove of memorabilia. Numerous bits and pieces from the family's past. A lock of hair, personal papers, letters, old photographs—the majority in sepia and attached to heavy cardstock.

"I'm not sure who these people are," Mae said from her seat beside Claire. "Probably friends or distant relatives. There's no way of knowin' without names on 'em. The family we can identify are in that album back there." She motioned to the bookcase behind them. "I couldn't bring myself to throw these away, though. They meant somethin' to someone once, otherwise they wouldn'ta kept 'em. So I kept 'em, too."

Claire touched the lock of chestnut hair. It was tied with a scrap of faded blue ribbon. "Do you know who this belonged to?" she asked quietly. Mae shook her head. "The ribbon's faded about the same as this." She lifted an old-fashioned greeting card on which a posy, a bird and an old-style wooden bucket were poised on a cottage window ledge overlooking a garden. The flower stems were held with a real pink ribbon tied into a flat bow. An inscription on the card's reverse, written in beautiful flowing script, said, *Never forget the days we spent together as children at the old home place.* It had been signed with a flourish by someone named Harry.

"Harry was my grandmother's older brother who stayed in Virginia," Mae explained. "Maybe the lock of hair is his. I remember seein' her in a rockin' chair, an old woman like me now, holdin' this card and pressin' the curl to her cheek like she was remembering someone she loved. But then, I can't say. She had this color hair, too, when she was young. At least, it looks brown in her picture."

"You have a picture of your grandmother?" Claire did her best not to sound overawed.

"Get me that big album from back behind us and I'll show it to you. But first—"

She dug a little deeper in the box and pulled out the framed sampler. She passed it to Claire. The aged linen was worked in bright silk thread and each stitch had been placed with care.

"My daddy liked it so much he hung it on the wall behind his desk. When Mama died he put it away, though. Said it hurt too much to look at every day. Wasn't long before he went, too, so he didn't have to pine for her for too long."

Claire retrieved the photo album. Mae rested it on her lap and turned to an early page. "This is my grandmother. Her name was Sue." She pointed to an unsmiling young woman posed stiffly in a chair, her elbow resting on a scarf-covered table.

As she studied the photograph, Claire was surprised at how youthful the young woman appeared, considering the terrible difficulties she'd faced in West Texas.

"This was taken around the time she and her parents settled around Dallas. In a year or two they moved farther west, as land opened up. I don't know how or where she and Gibson met up, but they did."

"She looks strong, even here," Claire said.

Mae laughed shortly. "She had to be! Have you started readin' that history book, or were you just lookin' at the pictures?"

"I've read the first two chapters."

"Then you'll know what I'm sayin'. The women had to be just as tough as the men."

"Is this Gibson?" Claire asked, pointing to another sepia photograph. The man might have been an older version of Rafe. He had the same chiseled features, dark eyes and fierce expression. He was somewhere in his seventies, his hair white, his skin brown and leathery.

"That's him," Mae confirmed. "And that's Virgil." She pointed to another photo.

Virgil bore a strong resemblance to his brother. He, too, was older and was seated next to a woman

of equal age. She wore what must have been an
unaccustomed frilly dress made of dark taffeta,
with tiny pleats running down the bodice and
sleeves. Her streaky white hair had been caught on
top her head in a style very similar to Mae's, but
the deeply etched lines on her face and the look in
her eyes spoke volumes about hard work and dep-
rivation.

"That's Deena, Virgil's wife. And this is Martha, my mother." Mae turned a page and pointed
to a young woman in her early twenties, wearing
a light-colored dress. Her features were soft, less
severe, and she was seated in a more relaxed manner in a chair beside a young man, also in his early
twenties. He stood a little behind her, his hand on
her shoulder. He, too, had the strong Parker look.
"That's my daddy, Watt," Mae murmured.

Claire gazed at the people from so long ago,
then grappled with the idea that the other pages
completing the thick album were also filled with
Parker relations.

Mae took her silence as encouragement. She
turned to a family tree affixed to the inside page
of the front cover. "You can see here how we're
descended from Gibson and Sue. Virgil and Deena
had two sons, but neither stuck on the ranch after
the first generation. My dad had two brothers, but
they moved on as well. That's why there's Parkers

in various parts of the state now, but each and
every one gets a share in the ranch when they turn
twenty-one. The Parkers on the ranch, except me,
all come from my brother, Jeff. I never married.
Never took the time. And my older brother Theodore—'' She turned instinctively to a page a little
deeper into the album, where a good-looking Parker male stood with other young men wearing
World War I uniforms. ''He died at the end of the
war. No marriage, no kids, either. Never had the
chance. I was barely more than a baby when it
happened, but I remember him.''

Claire's chest was tight. She felt overwhelmed
by everything she'd seen and heard...by the sadness that roughened Mae's voice when she spoke
of her long-deceased elder brother.

She did her best to steady herself, but couldn't.
She lurched to her feet, knowing that she needed
desperately to be on her own. ''Would you mind
if I— The bathroom—''

Mae instantly castigated herself. ''You just got
here and I keep *rushin'* things at you. Go...go!''
She waved Claire on her way. ''There's a bathroom in that upstairs room of yours, in case you
didn't notice it earlier. Use that instead of the one
down here, then get yourself a little rest without
worryin' about people watching you. I won't go

anywhere. I'll sit right here and keep lookin' at this.'' She patted the photo album.

Claire suffered a pang of conscience for making Mae Parker think herself culpable. Still, it got her out of the room.

She mumbled her thanks and hurried upstairs. In the bathroom she'd missed earlier, she splashed cold water on her face, then went to stretch out on one of the single beds. She *had* to regain control of herself But her insides twisted even tighter.

A family. Mae Parker had asked if she wanted a family.

Turning her head, Claire looked outside. From where she lay she could see scattered white clouds drifting across the cobalt blue sky.

Once, she'd wanted a family so badly she'd invented one for herself. A husband, two children... her.

Claire's eyelids fluttered shut.

She hadn't let herself think of the Fitzgeralds this openly for years. She'd banished them from her conscious mind as ruthlessly as she'd forbidden herself not to fraternize with her clients. She'd made that mistake once, she wouldn't do it again. It had hurt far too much.

Bryan, Fiona, Sean and Sara...the names still had the power to wound.

Shortly after she turned eighteen, she'd come to

their home to care for Fiona Fitzgerald. Not as a
nurse, but as home care help. To do all the little
things the woman was incapable of doing herself.
For years Bryan had done the best he could, working eight hours a day then coming home to care
for his children and his wife. He was a wonderful
man, and the children were everything Claire had
ever dreamed of. They were sweet and brave in the
face of their mother's degenerative illness. And
Fiona herself was sweet and brave....

It had been easy to let herself take on more re-
sponsibilities in her desire to help during the latter
months of Fiona's struggle, easy to slip into thinking herself one of them, easy to let her admiration
for Bryan turn into something deeper....

Claire had stayed on even after Fiona needed the
full services of a nurse, taking the children to the
park in the afternoons, ironing Bryan's shirts,
cooking their meals, listening—always listening—
when they needed to talk.

She'd let herself dream that when the inevitable
happened—as everyone knew it would—she'd stay
on with them, caring for them. And eventually she
and Bryan would marry, and the children would
look to her, as they already somewhat did, as a
mother—

It hadn't happened that way. Several days after
Fiona died, Bryan had called her into the living

room, thanked her from the bottom of his heart for
all her kindnesses, and given her a severance
check. He'd been generous. But he hadn't given
her what she wanted most.

He planned to start a new life, he'd said. Planned
for the children to start a new life. He would move
his family out of state.

Claire moaned. His words had devastated her.

Did she want a family? Mae had asked.

The Parkers knew so much about themselves…whereas she knew nothing.

She had no idea who her grandparents were, or
her great-grandparents. Or even her parents. She'd
just turned up one day in a box on the hood of a
car in an alley in Corpus Christi, Texas, about two
days old, with no note or identification. A search
had been carried out for her mother, but it had
turned up nothing.

Claire drew a ragged breath.

She repeated Mrs. Stanton's maxim like a mantra. "What a person doesn't have, they don't miss.
What a person doesn't have, they don't miss."

And she tried very hard to mean it.

CHAPTER SEVEN

CLAIRE SPENT A RESTLESS NIGHT. She dreamed fitfully of the Fitzgeralds. Of the children as children, instead of in their early twenties as they would be now. She dreamed of Mae and the other Parkers she'd met since coming to the ranch. She even dreamed herself back in time with Gibson and Sue when they were under attack from hostile forces. Then Rafe and Jodie appeared and accused her of being a hostile force!

At dawn's first pale light she threw the bedcovers off, donned her robe and slippers, then, after insuring that Mae still slept, set off in search of a glass of orange juice. When she was a child, someone was always sitting her down and handing her orange juice at disturbing moments. It had calmed her then and, by association, she hoped it still would today.

She padded through the dimness of the living room and dining room, found a glass in a kitchen cabinet and was about to open the refrigerator when bright light flooded the room.

It was impossible to say who was most startled—Claire, who'd heard no one enter, or Marie, who stood with one hand on the light switch and the other clutching her chest.

"Oh, my heaven, it's you!" the housekeeper exclaimed. "You coulda give me a heart attack!"

"I'm sorry, I didn't mean—"

"I'm not used to anyone bein' up this time of mornin'. You scared the life outta me!"

"I'm sorry," Claire apologized again.

The housekeeper sent her a suspicious look. "Just what were you doin', anyway? Lookin' for somethin' to eat?"

"Some orange juice actually, but—"

Marie brushed her aside and extracted a jug from the refrigerator. "Will this do?" she asked "It's fresh squeezed yesterday."

"Oh, yes," Claire said, and looked longingly at the jug. She needed the calming influence of the juice now more than ever.

Marie filled the glass.

"Thank you," Claire said softly, and took a long sip. "It's delicious."

"Just juice."

The woman's flat reply reminded Claire of yesterday, when they'd had a similar exchange about a glass of water.

She tried to smile. She knew she needed to take

advantage of this chance meeting to further ame-
liorate their relationship, but she didn't have the
energy. Not after her unsettled night.

"May I take this with me to the bedroom?" she
asked, lifting the glass.

"Sure," the woman said.

Distant laughter floated in through the open
kitchen window.

"That's the hands," Marie explained, tipping
her head toward the work area. "Axel's got 'em
fed and they're startin' their day."

"They begin early," Claire said.

"Lots to do on a ranch."

Claire longed to go back to the parlor, but Marie
had freely extended their conversation. Maybe this
was her way of telling Claire she wanted to start
fresh. Perching on a nearby stool, Claire took another sip of orange juice.

"It—the ranch—is quite large, isn't it?" she
asked.

"One of the bigger ones in West Texas."

Claire watched as the housekeeper placed a large
bowl and a rolling pin on the counter, then set
about gathering a canister of flour and an array of
other ingredients.

"I've read how the ranch started," Claire said.
"The brothers who came here."

"Took lots of grit to make this place what it is. By those in the past and those today."

"You've been with the Parkers a long time?" Claire ventured.

Marie shot her a long look. "Axel and me both have."

"Mae...Miss Parker...said—"

Marie turned away, her shoulders hunching. "I better get on with these biscuits."

Her unconscious use of their employer's first name had lost her ground, Claire realized. She was trying to figure out how to regain it, when the back door opened and Axel stepped inside.

His expression was comical when he spotted the two women. His first instinct looked to turn tail and run, but instead he greeted Claire a little too exuberantly. "Mornin'! How you doin'? Didn't expect to see you up so early. It's usually just Marie and me rattlin' around in the main house at this time a' day."

Claire secured the lapels of her robe, but as she did she smiled. She liked Axel. It was hard not to. "I woke up early," she explained.

"Came huntin' for juice," Marie expanded, the delivery flat.

Axel nodded and waited.

Finally Claire stood up. She'd made some headway, then lost some. All in all, though, she felt there'd been a little progress. "I should get back. Miss Parker might be waking. Thank you for the juice, Mrs.—" For the life of her she couldn't remember the couple's last name, and she didn't want to use Marie's given name unless invited.

"Call me Marie," the woman said brusquely. "Everyone else does."

"And I'm Axel." Axel grinned. "Wouldn't know who you were talkin' to if you called me Mr. Douglas."

Claire finished the remainder of her juice, then took the glass to the sink and rinsed it. Marie watched her with a sideways look.

As she passed Axel on her way into the dining room, he dipped his head infinitesimally to show approval.

"YOU'RE LOOKIN' CHIPPER," Mae said, her gaze following Claire as she retrieved a handkerchief from the chest of drawers. "You must be feelin' better today."

"I am," Claire agreed.

The matriarch sat up in bed. "Then you won't mind if we have another morning confab. I want you to tell me about that little get-together at Shannon's place yesterday. Jodie let it slip that you'd been there when she and Christine stopped by to see me afterward. You never said a word! I thought about askin' last night, but decided not to. You looked like you'd had more than enough for one day.'' Mae paused. ''What'd y'all talk about? Me?''

Claire returned with the requested handkerchief. ''Isn't that what you'd expect?'' she asked.

Mae snorted. ''Of course. What else did you talk about?''

''I didn't stay very long.''

''They still givin' you a hard time?''

''Not really. They were very nice.''

''As well they should be,'' Mae said tartly.

''I saw Gib's painting of Rafe,'' Claire volunteered, aiming again for distraction. ''He's named after your grandfather, isn't he? He's a very good artist.''

''Yeah, he's good,'' Mae conceded gruffly. ''And he is named after his great-granddaddy.''

Claire tilted her head. ''You don't consider him an accomplished artist? I thought—''

''Of course I do!'' Mae interrupted, twitching her legs under the cover.

''Then why did you say it the way you did?''

Mae took a moment to answer. ''It's hard havin' to admit you done someone wrong. And I did...with Gib. Made him hide his paintin' for years. Made him feel bad about it—when I knew all along what he was doin'." She paused again. "A coupla years back I asked him to paint ranch headquarters. He did, and now every time I look at it, tears come to my eyes, it's so pretty."

"Have you told him that?" Claire pressed gently. She could feel the woman's sincere regret.

"I've thanked him for it."

The curt answer warned off further inquiry, but Claire refused to be daunted. "Is that enough?" she asked.

The dark eyes flashed. "Of course it's not enough! But just as I was about to try to fix things up, he brought that woman to the ranch. Next thing, he tells me he wants to marry her! At his age! He's sixty-seven!"

Claire settled in the bedside chair. Their talk this morning could go on a while. "And there's something wrong with that?" she prompted carefully.

Mae scowled. "He probably met her in a bar, just like he did Jodie's mom. And look how that ended up! Ruby was a gold digger from the word go. She traded Gib and little Jodie for money just as soon as I offered it to her. She never loved him. Just like I doubt this one does, either. Gib doesn't understand how some people are happy to take advantage. He's *never* understood that. And now that he's successful, it's even worse." She eyed Claire. "That's one of the things I told you about—some-

thin' I'll need your help doin'. Gib has to be pro-
tected from himself. And Jodie's no help. She says
all she wants is for her daddy to be happy. And
that if this Lurleen woman makes him happy, it's
good enough for her.''

She waited for Claire to comment.

''If he's determined to marry her,'' Claire said
reasonably, ''what can you do?''

Mae smiled darkly. ''Oh, there's lots I can do.
You just watch. But somethin' else needs doin'
first. I want you to drive into Del Norte and pick
up some house plans I have waitin'. They've been
ready for a week, but I didn't want anyone here
knowin' what I'm up to.'' She motioned for Claire
to lean closer. ''It's the house I want to build Marie
and Axel. I've heard Marie talk, and it's exactly
what she wants. Hard part's gonna be gettin' 'em
to accept it, though.''

Claire sat back, surprised. ''Your family would
object? Is that why you don't want them to
know?'' From her short acquaintance with the
Parkers, they didn't strike her as stingy.

Mae looked at her as if she were crazy. ''*Where*
do you keep comin' up with things like that?'' she
demanded. ''I couldn't tell 'em, because they'd
start to worry. They'd think I was—'' She stopped
short, then repeated tightly, ''I couldn't tell 'em.''

Her expression cleared slowly. "But now you're here, it's time to do what's needed."

At last Claire understood. Even with Mae's larger-than-life personality, she was no different from Claire's previous charges. She sensed her time nearing and she wanted to put things right with the world around her. Only Mae was fiercely determined to do it her way, on her terms.

It was important to proceed carefully, Claire knew. "Don't you think talking to your family would be a good idea? They're all very concerned about you."

"I know how to handle my family," Mae snapped.

Claire sighed to herself. The woman was stubborn.

"When do you want me to leave for town?" she asked.

"That's more like it!" Mae approved, smiling broadly. "I'll call my lawyer and tell him you're comin'. He's been doin' me a favor by holdin' on to the plans. Anytime after breakfast will be fine."

Claire could only nod.

THE HORSE TANNER RODE lurched sideways, stumbling slightly on the uneven ground. Rafe, at his side, didn't bother to direct his horse out of the way. The horse sensed the movement himself and corrected for it.

"It's all comin' back, isn't it?" Rafe asked, his dark eyes assessing Tanner's "seat." "You look like you're doin' okay to me. You haven't forgot a thing."

Tanner wasn't about to admit to any sore places. He grinned. "Just like getting back on a bike."

"If we could've had you for a few more weeks those summers you visited, you might've grown into a pretty good cowboy. At least *you* were interested."

Rafe's reference was aimed at Tanner's only brother. Tanner shrugged. "Paul was always more into bugs. A horse put him too far up from the ground."

Rafe shook his head. "Bugs!"

"Turned out okay." Tanner smiled. "He's just won an award in College Station for his research on fire ants. Maybe he'll be the one to figure out how to control them."

"Now, that'd be a good thing." Rafe warmed to the possibility.

"Mom's proud of him," Tanner said.

Rafe glanced across the short distance that separated them. "She's proud of you, too. And the girls. She writes us every so often, keepin' us up with the news. Sophia's working on her third baby, isn't she?''

Tanner nodded. "She sure is."

"And she's livin' in London?''

"That's her.''

"And little Rhea?''

"She's in New York, going to school. Ginny's up in Minnesota.''

Rafe again shook his head. "You kids sure are scattered. Must be hard gettin' to see each other.''

"It's been a while since we've all been in the same place at the same time. Several years, in fact.''

"You probably found it hard to get away from your business.''

"Yes...I did." Tanner felt Rafe's quick estimating glance. He'd thought of Danny and his throat had automatically tightened.

"What are you plannin' to do with yourself on down the road? Get back into the computer business or look for somethin' different?'' Rafe chuckled. "I guess with money not bein' a problem, you don't have to *do* anything. You're a little on the young side to retire completely, though.''

"I'll do something," Tanner said, but he heard the indecision in his own voice.

"You just don't know what," Rafe surmised.

"No."

"You're welcome to hang out here as long as you want. We can always use another hand. Kinda different from what you're used to doin', but a lot more satisfyin'."

"I liked what I did," Tanner stated. At least, he once had.

He thought of the business he and Danny had built together. Of the way Danny had one day half-seriously told him his idea. Tanner had instantly grasped the possibilities, and within a month the newly fledged encryption software company had been formed. Danny coded and implemented the program, Tanner handled the finances and sales. An equal partnership in every way. A partnership that three years of immensely hard work had turned into a "hot" property employing a number of people in the heart of California's Silicon Valley. Clients had come to them, anxious for the capabilities their software provided for transactions over the Internet. Then the time had come when a major security corporation made an offer to buy the company, and after weeks of exhausting negotiations, a deal had been struck.

Tanner swallowed, his thoughts leaping ahead to what happened next. Nothing relieved his feelings of helplessness as he'd watched Danny fight for life. Or erased what Elaine said afterward. He lived it again and again.

"I've got that computer ordered." Rafe broke what must have been a long silence. "Should be able to sneak it into the ranch office by the end of this week. Then you can get started."

Tanner had a hard time shedding his memories. "Sure," he said distantly.

Rafe said nothing more.

As his mind cleared, Tanner wondered if their shared "mother" had written to Rafe, telling him of her concern.

He'd been far from his usual self upon returning to Phoenix. And he hadn't been able to talk about what had occurred, beyond the fact that Danny had died. He'd kept everything else inside. Suffered the blame, taken the guilt to heart.

The horses trudged on.

For a time Tanner felt a pressure inside himself to break the ongoing silence. To unburden his pain to this man—this near second brother—he'd admired for so long. But he couldn't do it. The emotional distance that continued to separate them was too great.

Then the silence that he remembered from his past visits to this expansive rugged land seeped into his soul, and for the first time since leaving California, Tanner found a measure of peace.

CLAIRE HAD NO DIFFICULTY locating the law office. Mae had told her it was directly across the street from the Del Norte courthouse, and that was exactly where it was. She parked in one of the angled slots and stepped into a nicely appointed waiting room. After a moment's conversation, the receptionist handed her a long cardboard cylinder that contained the house plans.

On her way out the door, Claire had a sudden thought to call Dr. Stevens. The friendly receptionist furnished both the phone and a slim telephone directory upon her return.

"Sure. Stop by," the doctor said pleasantly. "I can carve out a few minutes. That is, if you don't mind some hard looks from the folks in the waiting room."

"A few minutes would be fine," Claire said. "I won't need more."

Tanner's tour of the town had proved handy after all, which must have been Mae's intention all along. Claire had come to realize that the woman didn't do anything without having thought it through for both immediate and far-reaching purposes.

As the physician warned, the waiting room held several patients, and all looked askance at Claire when she gave her name to the medical receptionist and was told to go straight through.

The doctor sat at his desk in his office, making

notations in a patient's file. He looked up when she hesitated in the doorway.

"That didn't take long," he said, breaking into a smile and motioning her to a chair. His open face and curly dark hair made him look almost boyish.

"I was at Fowler and Fowler law offices, retrieving something for Miss Parker, when I thought this might be a good time to talk to you. I had no idea I was coming into town again so soon."

"What can I do for you?" he asked, as she perched in the chair opposite him.

"Miss Parker's family is worried. They're wondering if she needs tests, and I'm wondering as well. I have no information. Miss Parker called my agency Friday afternoon, I arrived Sunday."

The doctor made a tepee with his fingers. "Mae refused to give your agency a full medical history?"

"I'm not sure if she refused, or if—" She stopped. She didn't want to cast aspersions on her agency even if they were deserved.

"Mae can be quite a force when she wants to be," he said.

"I'm learning that."

He tapped his fingers together, as if mulling over what to say. Finally, he answered. "Mae's already had tests, at least the ones I could get her to consent to." At Claire's look of surprise, he added dryly, "Obviously, she didn't tell you."

"No, she didn't," Claire said.

He shook his head. "She's a law unto herself, that one."

"And the outcome of the tests?" Claire murmured.

"Mild tachycardia, occasional arrhythmia. She's wearing out. Her heart's getting weaker, her kidneys are tired. She could live another year, or go tomorrow. I can't say."

"What about a pacemaker? One of the family asked."

"She wouldn't hear of it even if it was indicated. She won't take the pills I've prescribed."

"Should I try to convince her to take them?"

He laughed. "I'd give you a medal if you could! I've had a number of run-in's with her over the past fifteen years. She doesn't think much of doctors. The pills are really more for my peace of mind than her medical well-being. They might help a little, but…"

"Why haven't you discussed this with her family?"

"Because she's made it plain I'm not to. Again, maybe you can convince her otherwise."

Claire digested what she'd been told, then stood

up and extended her hand. "Thank you, Dr. Stevens. For everything."

He rose as she did and accepted the brief handclasp. "The Parkers are good people. They're tough and won't give an inch when they feel strongly about something, but you couldn't ask for more loyal friends. If you need me, call. I'll try to drop by when I get a chance. But I know your agency. I know they only work with good people. Mae's in safe hands."

"Thank you," Claire said.

He walked down the corridor with her and paused outside the last examination room. A light frown furrowed his brow. "How's that friend of yours? That man you were with in the emergency room."

"He's…all right. It was just a momentary—"

"Thing?" he supplied dryly when she experienced a sudden loss of words.

"Yes," she agreed, and hurried back through the waiting room, where, once again, she received another round of irritable glances.

TANNER HAD MADE HIMSELF scarce in the main house. He'd hung out in his spare time at Rafe's, eaten breakfast and lunch with the hands and spent a good portion of this day out on the range. But that evening he couldn't avoid dinner. Mae would question him if he did.

He showered in the private bath connected to his bedroom, then dressed in his regular clothes. If he paid a little more attention to the way he looked, it was only because he'd been so filthy for much of the day. He couldn't believe the amount of dust and grime cowboys had to put up with. Or how physically intensive their work was. Though one of the men was up in his seventies, the old cowboy didn't let a little thing like age slow him down. He hopped up and down off his horse with the same gusto as the younger men, was just as quick with a rope and had the strength to manhandle a young steer. The two missing fingertips on his right hand didn't seem to bother him, either. Or the fond teasing he constantly received.

Tanner rolled his right shoulder in an effort to relieve the aching muscles. He'd tried to work out regularly over the past couple of years, going to a gym not far from his office and running a couple of miles when he could fit it in. That was probably the only thing that kept him from being a seized-up heap in the corner right now, after his progression from ranch ''guest'' to the newest hand being shown the ropes.

He smiled. Literally, he'd been shown the ropes. Gene, the seventy-something-year-old, had taken on the chore of teaching him the basics of roping. He'd been awful, particularly in comparison with Gene.

"I been cowboyin' for over forty-five years, son," Gene had said bracingly. "Lassoin's how I lost these here two fingers. Got caught in the rope. An ornery steer give me this limp. Drove his horn straight inta my knee when I was younger'n you. Lemme tell you about it," he'd said, and had proceeded to do so for the next hour as he patiently gave Tanner pointers on catching an old tree stump with his loop. "Need ta practice," Gene had admonished him before they parted company for the day.

Tanner rolled his shoulder again as he stepped into the hall. He wondered what Claire had done with her day. Then he wondered why it should matter.

He came upon the two women in the living room—Claire sitting calm and unruffled on the couch, penciling something in a notebook, Mae reading a newspaper in a straight-backed chair.

Claire slipped the notebook into the skirt pocket of her trim-fitting dress. It must be some kind of uniform, Tanner figured. It was casual, but the same style as the others she'd worn. The only difference was the pastel color.

Mae looked him up and down. "I heard you were out fixin' fence today."

He smiled self-mockingly. "I tried."

"And that you caught on pretty quick!"

"Well, I'm learning the principles. I'm just not very good at it."

"Nobody starts out bein' good," she snapped. "Takes time."

His gaze returned to Claire. He felt Mae looking at him speculatively and pulled his eyes away.

"Also heard you're learnin' to use a rope," Mae continued. "That's good. Always a handy thing to know. Parker kids learn by the time they're four."

She folded the newspaper, tucked it under her arm and reached for her cane. "Well, now that you're here, I'll be off. The two of you enjoy your meal."

Claire lifted her head. "You're not eating with us?" she asked.

"No. Most days I take my lunch in my office. Today, I'm takin' dinner, too. I have some private calls to make."

The matriarch rocked twice to gain her feet. On the second try Claire and Tanner both reached to help her. She dismissed them with an irritable grunt.

"Would you like me to come with you?" Claire asked. "To see you settled."

"Nope. I'd rather do it myself." And she proceeded from the room with great dignity.

After a moment, Tanner remarked, "I suppose we should go in."

"Yes," Claire agreed.

They had a wide choice of seating at the massive table, but both took the chairs they'd used before.

Marie appeared in seconds. "We're havin' roast and vegetables tonight. If you don't mind, I'll get Miss Mae's dinner before I serve yours. Won't take a minute."

She'd gone before either of them could answer.

This time when Tanner's gaze settled on Claire, he let it linger.

She was so contained. So silent. Her skin soft and finely textured, her delicate features composed. She might have been a period painting sitting perfectly still across from him in her pale blue dress, or maybe an impressionistic watercolor. An ethereal entity just out of his reach. His hand lifted of its own accord....

"What's in the notebook?" he asked, dragging himself back to reality. He made the hand movement look planned by motioning toward her skirt pocket.

She shrugged. "Nothing much. I doodle."

"May I see it?"

"Why?"

"Because I'm curious."

Her gray eyes held his and he almost lost it again. Then she slid the notebook across the table.

Tanner hesitated. What had begun as a way to control his whimsical thoughts had progressed to something else. He felt like he was prying, but he couldn't stop himself. He flicked open the notebook's cover and was surprised by the credible pencil rendering of a water lily. He flicked to the second page, where, with simple strokes, she'd captured an overgrown pond.

"Very nice," he said.

"It passes the time."

He slid the notebook back to her. There were many more pages, but he couldn't trespass further.

"Have you met Gib Parker yet? He did that painting in the living room. The one of ranch headquarters. You've seen it?"

"Briefly," she replied.

"Rafe has one of his paintings in his house, too. Gib is his uncle."

"I've heard...and I've seen it." She changed the subject. "Tell me about throwing a rope."

"I know enough to doubt I'll ever be any good, no matter how often I practice. I think you have to be born to it."

"Didn't you say you're from Arizona? Not a ranch?"

"My dad's a home builder in Phoenix."

Marie saved them from more uncomfortable attempts at conversation by bustling into the room carrying a platter of steaming roast beef. Then she ferried in bowls of vegetables and a tray piled high with freshly baked rolls.

"Marie, you're a marvel," Tanner declared.

"Plenty more where this comes from, so don't hold back!"

The housekeeper's smile transformed her blunt features, and Tanner noticed Claire's surprise.

When they were once again alone, he confided, "See? The Grand Dragon's not so bad. Not once she decides you're not out to harm the Parkers."

"She probably considers you a Parker."

He sliced the roast with a wooden-handled knife. "Believe me, she doesn't. It took two visits for me to get in her good graces. She was polite to us kids, but not very approachable. She resented how Rafe's mom upset Mae when she married my dad."

"What changed after the second visit?"

"She's a sucker for kids. She and Axel both are. They don't have any of their own, so they kind of latch on to the ones around here."

"That makes her even more protective of the Parkers."

After checking what she wanted, he transferred

a thin slice of meat to her plate, then forked several onto his own.

"How's it going with the two of you?" he asked. "I noticed she didn't come after you with the knife." He waggled the carving knife before setting it aside.

She shrugged. "We're making progress."

"Good." He offered her the bowl of creamed potatoes before availing himself of a generous portion.

Table manners. Another thing to thank his stepmother for. Gloria had taken the little heathens the younger Reid children had become during their mother's illness and retaught them their manners.

Thanks, Gloria! he saluted her silently.

Claire had fastened her gaze on her plate and it seemed she intended it to stay there.

He would have to come up with something good to get her to look at him again.

CHAPTER EIGHT

CLAIRE APPLIED HERSELF to her meal with the idea that, shortly, she could excuse herself. But just as she was about to push away from the table, Tanner said something she couldn't respond to with a noncommittal *um* or *ah*.

"When Rafe's mother married my father it created a huge rift. Mae still hasn't forgiven her."

Mae had said something to that effect the day before, Claire recalled. Something about having "plainly" told Rafe's mother not to marry Tanner's father.

"How long has it been?" she asked.

"Rafe was nineteen. I was nine."

"Does she not like your father?"

"She'd never met him before the wedding."

Claire frowned. "Surely she had a reason."

"She didn't think it proper for Gloria to marry a man she'd just met on a cruise. She ordered her not to, but—" He grinned. "I guess my dad was very persuasive. He'd been widowed for eighteen months and all his friends kept pressuring him to take some time for himself. He finally booked his ticket for a Caribbean trip, went on it…and came home with a fiancée. Not even the prospect of five children, three to fifteen, scared Gloria off. Dad said neither of them meant for it to happen. They just saw each other, and—'' He shrugged.

So Tanner's father had lost his wife, just as Bryan Fitzgerald had lost Fiona. Had Bryan gone on a cruise a year or so later and found someone for himself and his children? Claire wondered.

She shook the painful thought away, then was angry with herself that it *was* still painful. What Bryan Fitzgerald had or hadn't done after he moved away from Corpus Christi didn't concern her. It hadn't concerned her then, either, except in her own mind.

Tanner continued, not knowing that each word cut deeply into her. ''It was the best thing that could've happened to us kids. Ginny, my oldest sister, did her best to keep us in order. But after Mom died, we sort of fell apart. Gloria put us together again.''

Claire pushed back her chair. She couldn't continue to listen to this.

Then once again, he halted her with a statement.

''Rafe refuses to telephone Gloria to tell her about Mae. He thinks that if he contacts her, he'll be admitting Mae's going downhill. *I'm* worried that if Gloria doesn't know, she might lose the chance to see her again.''

''Do you think she'd want to?'' Claire asked tightly.

''She loves Mae. It's not her choice that they're at odds.''

Claire had put the past behind her. Made a life she could be satisfied with. She helped people, performed a valuable service. She didn't want or need reminders that reopened the hurt.

''What are you asking me?'' she demanded.

His brown eyes were serious. ''I'm asking if you think *I* should call her.''

Claire didn't know what to say. ''I—I think you should do what you consider best. Now, if you'll excuse me—''

Head up, shoulders back—every inch the cool professional—she started from the room.

''Wait!'' he called after her.

She heard the legs of his chair scrape the floor.

''You've forgotten something.''

She turned.

He crossed the room, his hand extended. ''Your notebook,'' he said, smiling. ''You left it on the table.''

''Thanks,'' Claire murmured, taking it from him.

All she wanted was to get away, but her conscience made her meet his eyes. It wasn't his fault that his tale about his family had hit uncomfortably close to home for her.

Then she wished she had simply left. His slim, athletic body and boy-next-door good looks jolted her with a strong pull of attraction—one she instantly rejected!

Finally, turning on her heels, she fled the room.

OVER THE NEXT FEW DAYS Claire saw nothing of Tanner Reid—not because she chose to avoid him, but because he worked such long hours out on the ranch.

She, too, kept busy. At Mae's instruction, when the various members of her family stopped by the main house on their frequent visits, Claire remained at the matriarch's side.

The family's initial resistance to her presence at the ranch slowly eased. Most seemed to adjust to her being there. Undoubtedly, Mae's intent.

Claire finally met Gib Parker, a friendly man with an easy smile and manner. He shared the same look as the younger Parker men, though he carried more weight and his hair had gone almost completely white.

She also met the children who called the compound home. LeRoy and Harriet's teenagers, Wesley and Gwen. Wes, a young man of eighteen, lean and rangy, barely said a word in her presence. Gwen, nearly sixteen, had her mother's wide-spaced gray eyes and sweet smile. Then there was Anna, their nine-year-old sister, and eight-year-old Ward and seven-year-old Nate—Rafe and Shannon's boys. "Typical Parker males," as Shannon had described them. The boys' younger sister, Nikki, was not yet two.

The Parker children were an interesting mix. Claire could see that the family traits of fierce determination and unpretentiousness had carried over into the next generation.

Upon awakening early on Saturday morning, Claire learned that ranch work was a seven-day-a-week operation. It didn't stop for weekends.

Perched on the kitchen stool while Marie made biscuits, she once again heard the cowboys start their day.

Marie paused to look out the window. "Sure surprises me how Tanner's taken to ranch work."

Claire didn't know whether to be pleased or displeased at the spurt of electricity that ran through her body when she heard his name. That it was merely a "spurt" was good.

"Why would that surprise you?" she asked. The housekeeper had continued to unbend each day, becoming almost friendly. When Claire entered the kitchen earlier, Marie had filled a glass with orange juice and offered it to her.

"I just didn't think he had it in him," Marie said as she went back to cutting biscuits. "He was always more into books. Use to bring a whole bunch of 'em with him when he visited as a boy."

"What was he like as a boy?" Claire asked, then wondered why it should matter to her.

Marie shot her a curious look. "Quiet," she said after a minute.

A companionable silence fell between them. With ease of practice, Marie transferred rounds of biscuit dough onto a cooking tray, covered it with a fresh dish towel, then slid it to one side on the counter.

"Miss Parker's told Axel and me to come see her in her office after breakfast this mornin'. You got any idea what it might be about?" the housekeeper asked as she gathered used implements and took them to the sink.

Claire did have a good idea. Mae probably planned to broach the subject of the prospective house. But she pretended puzzlement. "She rarely speaks to the two of you together?"

"She *never* does. It's always him or me, about somethin' she wants done."

"Maybe that's what it is this time," Claire suggested.

"Only thing the two of us do together is the barbecues. Axel cooks the meat and the dessert and sets up the tables. I do everythin' else. But that couldn't be it. Nothin' new to tell us about that. We can do one a' those in our sleep."

Claire shrugged and remained silent.

"She's restin' more these days than she used to." Marie frowned. "Time was when she didn't stop goin' from dawn till midnight. Kept busy all the time. Even went out on roundups and helped with the brandin'."

"I've heard she rode into her eighties."

"She went ridin' on her eightieth birthday. Pretty well had stopped before that, though, when she broke her leg. That's also about the time she turned the full runnin' of the ranch over to Rafe. Both were hard things for her to do. She loved to ride and she loved bein' in charge."

Claire smiled slightly. "From what I've seen so far, she's *still* in charge."

"Oh, she's that, all right," Marie agreed. "Not so much of the ranch—her and Rafe locked horns for some time about that. He makes those decisions now, and she only butts in when she thinks it's important."

"Like with the ranch records."

Marie nodded. "She's in charge of the family. They don't enjoy it much when she stirs things up. Never have. They fuss, but she almost always wins." Her words turned gruff as she grew sentimental. "She only does it 'cause she loves 'em so much. They know that, even when they're fightin' her the hardest." The pain in the housekeeper's voice drew Claire to her side. She gently rested a hand on the woman's arm.

Moisture beaded Marie's lashes when she looked up. "I know she's old and that she can't go on forever...but I wish she could. I sure wish she could!"

In the past Claire would have offered some kind of platitude that was sympathetic yet distancing. In this instance, though, she couldn't do it. The words wouldn't come.

"I gotta stop thinkin' like that, though," Marie said, taking a deep breath. "Miss Mae can sense things. I don't want her seein' me all blubbery again." She looked at Claire. "You do this kinda thing all the time, don't ya? You're good at keepin' people from seein' what's inside you—the ones you take care of." She paused to consider. "I don't know how you do it."

Marie ran warm water in the bowl and began to scrub it energetically. "I just want you to know...I'm sorry for the way I treated you when you first got here. I was wrong. It's probably best for her to have someone from outside. Those of us livin' here…we love her too much to keep our feelin's back.''

At last Claire broke her silence. ''When I arrived, you said something—''

''I've apologized,'' Marie inserted quickly.

''No, it's not that. It's— Miss Parker doesn't blame you for what happened.''

The housekeeper tensed.

Claire went on. ''She didn't hire me because of anything you did or didn't do. It's what you said just now. She did it out of consideration for all of you. I'm not a part of the family. You are.''

''Axel and me aren't Parkers,'' Marie denied.

''Yes, you are,'' Claire countered simply, causing the housekeeper to sniff.

When she returned to the bedroom parlor, Claire wondered if she'd done the right thing. It seemed right. The loyal housekeeper shouldn't suffer for an imagined slight. And if Mae was going to spring the building plans on the couple, Marie might put up less resistance if the way was paved.

LATER THAT MORNING Mae awakened her usual self, although at breakfast she was taciturn. It was only as Claire accompanied her to her office that she related her plans for the morning—the upcoming meeting with the Douglases, as well as a meeting with the private investigator she'd sent to check up on Gib's new girlfriend.

"An investigator?" Claire echoed, quick to close the hall door. She doubted Mae would want the conversation overheard.

The matriarch lifted her chin. "I've used him before. He does a good job. Thorough without being obtrusive."

Claire frowned. "Does your nephew know what you're doing?"

"No."

"But—"

"I don't have time to pussyfoot around," she asserted crisply. "I want to get the goods on her, and I don't care what anybody says."

"If the investigator comes to the ranch, won't you be taking the chance that Gib—"

"That's where you come in," Mae cut in smoothly. "I want you to keep him busy. He spends most mornings in that shed he calls a studio, but just as soon as I count on him doin' it today, he'll walk in at the wrong time. He knows John Fellows. Knows what he does for me. It won't take him long to put two and two together."

"Are you planning to tell him what you learn?"

"Sure I am, but when I'm ready."

Someone tapped on the door and Mae called out entry.

Marie and Axel stepped into the room, both looking anxious.

Mae promptly set everyone a task. "Axel, Marie…sit yourselves down. Claire, go get that tube out of my bedroom closet."

"We'll stand," Marie stated solemnly.

"No, I want you to sit," Mae repeated. "Claire…?"

Claire didn't wait for another directive. She hurried to the bedroom, found the tube from the lawyer's office in Mae's closet and returned to the others. Mae sat like a queen on the couch, bracketed by the Douglases.

"Help me hold this," she muttered to Claire as she attempted to unroll the plans on the low table.

Marie looked at the drawings and frowned. "What is it?"

"It's a house," Mae answered. "Your house. The one I want to build for you."

"A house?" Axel repeated, looking stunned.

Mae showed off her handiwork. "It's got everything you want, Marie. A breakfast nook, double sinks in the bathroom, big closets, lots of space in the kitchen…."

"Are you firin' us?" Marie asked hollowly.

"No! I want you to keep doin' what you're

doin'. But you should have a place of your own." She motioned to the land around them. "You pick the spot. Up close to the compound, if you want, so you don't have far to walk."

The couple looked at each other blankly, then turned back. "But we like livin' in the main house," Marie said.

"You'll like havin' your own place better. I've heard you talk about your dream house for years, Marie. There's even a walk-in pantry!"

Marie sat stock-still while Axel peered tentatively at the plans.

"We can't let you do it," Marie objected. "It wouldn't be right."

"It's right if I say it's right!" Mae shot back. "You two have earned it. Look on this as your retirement place."

"We don't want to retire."

"You may not now, but you will later."

Marie continued to shake her head.

Axel cleared his throat. "Not that we aren't mighty grateful—"

"If you're *grateful,* you'll do what I say!" Mae snapped, her irritation growing.

The couple looked at Claire.

Claire wished Mae had dismissed her after she'd retrieved the architectural plans. This was private business for the three of them. Surely Marie resented her presence. But as she studied both Marie and Axel, she could see their concern was only for Mae.

"Maybe they'd like to think about it," Claire proposed, hoping to be of help.

Marie seized on the suggestion. "Yes! Let us think about it. Like Axel said, we *are* grateful."

Mae fretted, then finally agreed. "All right. You do that. Just don't forget I want you to have it!"

The couple looked no less anxious when they stood up to leave than they had when they'd entered.

"Here, take the plans with you," Mae called out, stopping them. "Study 'em. See if there's anythin' you want changed, anythin' at all. You just have to say." She tried to force the plans back into the cylinder, but ended up pushing the collection to Claire.

Claire allowed the drawings to roll naturally, tightened them, then stuffed them into the tube. With her back to Mae, she handed it to the couple and offered what she hoped was an encouraging smile.

Once the Douglases left, Mae looked at her steadily.

"You think I pushed 'em too hard?" she demanded.

"Possibly a little," Claire answered honestly.

"Didn't exactly go the way I planned."

"They were stunned."

"Shoulda done it different," Mae grumbled, and crossed to her desk. She fixed Claire with a brooding gaze as she sat down. "John'll be here at eleven-thirty. That's when I need you to go see Gib. Marie'll tell you which shed is his."

"Do I have a reason for going to see him?" Claire asked. She was sure Mae had already thought one up.

"I've seen you drawin' in that notebook you carry. Take it along and show it to him. Tell him you're interested in his work. That'll keep him goin' for a time." Then, as if suddenly worn down, she brusquely dismissed Claire. "Now, get goin' yourself, and don't come back until after John's been and gone. I have to make a call."

Claire was concerned about the woman's sudden weariness. "Maybe you should rest," she suggested.

"Got too much to do," Mae snapped as she reached for the phone.

Yet when Claire turned to close the door after stepping into the hall, she heard the handset settle back on the receiver. Mae had not completed dialing.

Once she returned to the bedroom parlor, Claire took a moment to catch her breath. After her productive meeting with Dr. Stevens, she'd been of two minds whether to tell Mae what she'd learned. In the end, she decided to leave things as they were. The only difference her knowledge might make would be to add medical authority to her instructions that her client get more rest. Not that it would influence Mae any!

Claire checked her watch. She needed to keep a close eye on the time.

"IT'S LOVELY," CLAIRE SAID with genuine admiration as she gazed at a painting of an old cowboy gifting a toddler with a wildflower. The cowboy was dressed in his well-worn working clothes and wearing a hat that might have matched his grizzled years. Bending deeply at the waist, the man grinned as he delicately extended the flower to a little girl with bright copper-colored hair. The child echoed his stance and their fingers met on the stem.

"That's Gene, one of our hands, and Megan, my grandbaby," Gib said proudly. "I painted it for Jodie and Tate. Thought they might enjoy it."

That painting wasn't the only likeness of the little girl in the crowded studio.

Gib grinned. "I kinda like paintin' her."

"How old is she?" Claire asked.

"Gonna be two in September."

"Is she your only grandchild?"

"Only one. Just like Jodie's my only daughter."

"I've met Jodie," Claire said.

"So I heard."

Claire looked up from inspecting another painting of the child to see that his gaze matched his teasing tone.

"Heard she was a little hard on ya," he continued. "You'll understand better if you know that Mae practically raised her. The two of them..." He shook his mostly white head. "Jodie's the closest Mae's ever come to havin' a baby of her own, and Mae's the closest Jodie's ever had to havin' a mama after her real one took off."

Claire lifted another painting. A landscape. "This one's nice, too," she said.

"I did that a few years back. It's out in Red Canyon Division."

He brought out more landscape canvases for Claire to see. Not to boast, but to show her different aspects of the ranch. As in his previous paintings, his subjects seemed to come to life. The animals, the cowboys, the awesome isolated beauty of the land.

"A cowboy who paints," Claire mused softly. "I suppose that gives you some special insight?"

Gib seemed surprised. "Me?" He laughed. "I'm no cowboy. I'm not any good on a horse. Never have been, never will be."

"But I thought—"

"I was always at Mae's beck and call. Did what she wanted—drove her here or there, went to pick things up or take messages to people. Never was much good for anythin' else."

"But these—" Claire motioned to the canvases.

"Are the only thing I *can* do." He grinned again. "Don't bother me none, bein' useless most of my life. Used to bother Aunt Mae, but it doesn't seem to so much anymore. Not since she found out people like my work." He eyed Claire. "Seems like you took my place as her gofer. Isn't that what they're called? You off on one of her errands now?"

Claire hadn't expected such keen insight. She jumped slightly at being caught out.

"I've watched her work her ways enough times over the years to know when she's up to somethin'," Gib explained. "Only...I'm either gettin' good at spottin' it or she's losin' her touch." He sobered. "Hope it's me gettin' good."

"She told me to show this to you," Claire said, retrieving the notebook from her pocket.

Gib leafed through the pages with great care. "Not bad," he said kindly. "Is drawin' your hobby?"

"In my spare time. I don't like to watch TV."

"Me, neither," Gib agreed. "Big waste a' time.

Except for when they put on those old classic comedy movies.''

"I play at sketching," Claire admitted candidly. "I know I'm not very good."

"I never thought I was, either." He handed back the notebook. "Took years before I got brave enough to show my work to anybody."

Claire smiled. "There's a difference between a fine talent and just being adequate."

"Enjoyin' what you do is what counts. I'm never goin' to put most of these on the market. I do 'em 'cause I want to."

Claire felt an immediate link with this Parker. He wasn't as fierce or intimidating as his relatives. Then she remembered what Mae was doing at this moment and experienced a twinge of guilt at her part in facilitating it.

Gib eased back onto his seat before a work in progress. It, too, was a landscape. He dabbed his brush in a splash of burnt sienna on his palette and deftly applied it to an unfinished cliff side. "So, what's she up to today? Somethin' to do with me? Nah, don't answer," he said when Claire tensed again. "I think I got me an idea." He adjusted the line of his previous stroke and continued congenially. "Just so you know...I won't be movin' from this spot for a while. Probably be here most of the afternoon."

"Thank you for showing me your paintings," Claire murmured.

He turned dark Parker eyes on her. "Come back anytime you want," he said, and Claire sensed that he truly meant it.

CHAPTER NINE

"WHO WAS THAT LEAVING just now?" Jodie asked, straightening after releasing her daughter from the child's car seat. She and her family had arrived just as John Fellows's car pulled away.

Mae glanced at Claire, who seconds before had returned from Gib's studio. "Cut it kinda close, didn't ya?" she observed sotto voce. Then, projecting her voice, she addressed her great-niece. "Nobody that needs to concern you."

The redheaded toddler Claire had seen in Gib's paintings clambered up the short path onto the porch to hug her great-great-aunt's knee. Mae teetered, but smiled fondly and patted the bright head.

"Megan, be careful," Jodie directed as she hurried onto the porch.

Claire looked at the man bringing up the rear. Since the car they'd driven up in was a white police patrol car with a blue stripe down the side, lights across the roof and county insignia on both front doors, it didn't surprise her that he wore a uniform—a long-sleeved tan shirt, tan pants, a dark brown tie and a five-pointed Texas star above his shirt's left pocket flap. He also wore a service belt with a gun, and patches on each shoulder. Tall and slim, he had close-cropped brown hair, steady brown eyes and a face that gave nothing away. He returned her regard without blinking.

"Tate Connelly," he introduced himself.

"Claire Hannaford," she responded.

He moved past her to kiss Mae's cheek. "I'm not stoppin'," he said easily. "Gotta check on somethin' out at Mike Newman's place. Jodie—" his expression and his voice warmed as he spoke her name "—you'll find your way back to town? I'm not sure what all I'll be gettin' into over there."

Jodie's fingers lingered on his arm. "Dad will bring us in. He won't mind."

He transferred possession of the tote bag he carried to his wife, bestowed a light kiss on her upraised lips, ruffled his daughter's hair and turned to leave.

"Tate—" Mae called after him, causing him to turn around. "You take care, you hear?"

The earnestness of the older woman's tone seemed to disconcert both adult visitors. Tate fired a look at Jodie, half waved to Mae in acknowledgment, then continued to the patrol car.

Jodie's mouth tightened as she looked first at her great-aunt, then turned to watch her husband.

Tate's departure was further delayed when Rafe and Tanner came down the gravel drive, returning from the work area. Both men bore the morning's sweat and grime. Their clothes and hats were dusty, their boots scuffed. After greeting one another, the men exchanged a few words before Tate finally drove away, back on official time.

Claire had watched the sheriff's movements with interest. He looked to be fully recovered from the gunshot wounds Tanner had told her about.

Her gaze moved to Tanner. If anything, his unkempt state made him look even more attractive. His wide shoulders and slim hips were accentuated by snugly fitting jeans, his face... She *had* to stop reacting this way! Hadn't she caused herself enough problems in the past by weaving impossible fantasies? Did she want it to happen again? Her life had been grim for a long period as she'd worked to put the pieces back together.

When Tanner noticed her watching him, she looked away. She *had* to stay detached.

The yellow dog ran up on the porch, making the little girl shriek. Her shriek dissolved into giggles as he trotted straight over to her and, wagging his tail, tried to lick her fingers.

Mae smiled at the child and the dog, then glanced at the sun's position in the midday sky.

"You two callin' it quits already?" she asked the men.

Rafe propped a boot on the lower step, but didn't mount it to the porch as Tanner had. "I have some things to see to and Tanner's cut his arm." His black eyes flicked to Claire. "It could use a little professional attention."

For the first time Claire noticed the handkerchief wrapped around Tanner's forearm. "Of course," she said.

"It's just a scrape," Tanner claimed.

"Still needs to be seen to," Rafe ordered.

Mae sized up her guest. "Startin' to look like a real cowboy, Tanner. Suppose you can't help gettin' hurt like one when you do the work."

"Some barbed wire bit him," Rafe explained, then tapping the nearest wrought-iron porch post with his open hand, he glanced at his cousin. "You gonna be around for a while this afternoon, Jodie?"

"Sure," she said.

"Then I'll see you later," he stated, and set off for his house.

Mae herded everyone inside, where, in what Claire was coming to recognize as her usual way, she handed out assignments.

"Claire, you see to Tanner. There's a first-aid kit in the bathroom down the hall. Jodie, you and that little angel of yours come with me. I swear she's grown an inch since the last time I saw her. And it's only been a week."

Claire and Tanner stood in the entryway as the others moved away.

"The wound should be cleaned," Claire said, taking refuge in her training.

He unwound the handkerchief to reveal an angry scratch. "Stings like hell," he admitted, grimacing. "But I wasn't about to say it in front of them. These people would work with one leg cut off!"

Claire started for the bathroom and he followed her.

The small room felt far too constrictive even with the door open. Every time she moved as she searched for the first-aid kit, she bumped into him.

Finally, she located the kit and cleaned the wound with an antiseptic gauze...all the while trying not to notice that her fingers were unusually cold and near trembling.

"I hope that didn't hurt too much," she apologized stiffly once she finished.

"It hurt a lot less than when that barbed wire sprang back. It was like a snake. I stretched out a line the way Rafe showed me, and was trying to tack it to a post, when *whang!* It got me."

"Was it rusty?" she asked, busying herself with the selection of a proper-sized bandage. Anything to avoid looking at him.

"Probably. Been out in the weather for God-knows-how-long."

"Then you should get a tetanus booster. Lockjaw isn't something to play with. Not when preventing it is so easy. Have you had a booster shot recently?"

She made the mistake of lifting her eyes.

He'd been leaning back against the sink the whole time she'd ministered to him. He hadn't moved, but something had changed. Awareness crackled in the air between them.

Claire jerked her attention back to the bandage. "We...we should apply this to protect the wound." She fumbled with the paper covering.

His hand covered hers, stopping her heart.

"No need," he said, his voice sounding even huskier. "I have to shower and change. I'm doing something for Rafe in his office after lunch."

Lunch! The two of them alone again! Claire racked her brain for an excuse Mae would believe. Then she remembered that Jodie was here. In all likelihood, Mae would invite her to share the meal and be present herself.

She extended the mangled but still unopened bandage. "Use it after your shower," she said levelly, hoping that nothing she felt had been revealed in her words. "And don't forget your shot. I'm sure Dr. Stevens would be happy to do it for you."

She slipped the kit back into the drawer and edged into the hallway. From there, she smiled tightly and hurried off...in the wrong direction. Instead of turning down the hall toward the parlor, she'd headed up the hall, to the front of the house.

There was nothing she could do but turn into the living room. She couldn't go upstairs, because that was where Tanner was going. And if she retraced her steps, she would have to pass him.

The two Parker women shared one of the couches. Claire hesitated in the doorway. Ordinarily, she'd never intrude on their conversation. But since Mae had ordered her attendance in the past few days when she spoke with members of her family, Claire gave herself permission to enter.

Both women looked around as she seated herself in a chair a distance away, but neither raised an objection.

Jodie picked up their conversation where she must have left off. "So that *was* John Fellows I saw driving away. Why was he here?"

The little girl played at her feet, absorbed in trying to fit playing cards through a slit in the lid of a small plastic box.

"He was reportin' in to me," Mae said. "About something I asked him to do."

"What?" Jodie asked directly.

Mae lifted her chin. "It's none of your business, Missy. I have every right to check anything I want."

Jodie's eyes flashed. "You asked him to check up on Lurleen, didn't you? Why can't you just let Daddy be happy?"

"As old as he is, your daddy's still a man. And men don't always think with their brains."

"She's a nice woman, Aunt Mae. I've met her several times."

"People don't always show what they are. You know that."

"And sometimes they do," Jodie came back.

The toddler handed her mother a playing card. Jodie fitted it through the slit, and that became the game. The little girl handed her mother card after card, which Jodie automatically fitted in.

"So, did he learn anything?" Jodie demanded.

"He hasn't had enough time."

"Which means he didn't."

"It means 'not yet,'" Mae snapped.

The child looked from one woman to the other and seemed momentarily confused by their tense exchange. She moved to Mae and handed her a card. Mae took it, but didn't push it through the lid.

"Card, Mi-Mae," the child said, trying to get her aunt's attention.

"I told him to keep tryin'," Mae continued, not seeming to hear the girl. "Fort Stockton's big, but not that big. And it's his town...where he has his office."

"Mi-Mae!" the girl insisted in her clear sweet voice. She bumped the elderly woman's arm with the box. "Put card in, Mi-Mae!"

Mae looked around sharply, her gaze centering on Claire. "Take little Megan out to the kitchen to see Marie. Her mama and I need to talk."

"Will she come with me?" Claire asked, rising.

"Of course she'll come with you," Mae clipped. "Pick her up off her feet and she's gotta come!"

"But—"

Jodie stood up and, clearly irritated by the previous exchange, lifted her daughter, box and all. "I'll come with you," she said shortly. "Aunt Mae, I'll be back in a minute." Then she strode into the dining room ahead of Claire.

The sudden invasion of her kitchen took Marie by surprise. But after a quick wipe of her hands, she reached for the child.

Megan's troubled look disappeared instantly.

"Mrie! Card, Mrie!" she shrieked as she offered her the box.

The housekeeper kissed the child's soft round cheek and set her on the floor. Then she retrieved the cards from inside the box and slid several back through the slot, before offering the remainder to the happy little girl.

Jodie exhaled her frustration. "Aunt Mae makes me so angry sometimes! She's worried me half to death this past week, then she does something so—" She broke off when her daughter's brown eyes—the same dark caramel as her father's—lifted. Visibly calming herself, she continued, "I wanted to get back out here right away, but Emma's kept me so busy with that women's club fair she's roped me into helping with this year. Emma is Tate's mother," Jodie explained in an aside to Claire. "You aren't going to believe what Aunt Mae's doing this time, Marie. She's having Dad's fiancée investigated. Why can't she just let things be? He's not the same person he was when he went off and married my mother. He's brought Lurleen to the ranch, introduced her to everyone, even brought her to dinner with Tate and me and Megan—more than once. I don't know what more Aunt Mae wants!"

Of all the blood Parkers Claire had met, Jodie physically looked the least like them. With her flame-colored hair and gamine features, she could easily be mistaken—as Claire had mistaken her at first—for an in-law. But her fiercely intense personality validated the familial link.

"That's not all she's done," Marie said, ready to contribute her own information.

Jodie frowned and waited.

"She's had some plans fixed up for a house for Axel and me."

"A house?" Jodie echoed.

"A retirement place, as she puts it."

Jodie's frown disappeared. "That's not such a bad idea."

"We don't want a house. We want to stay right here."

"Does she plan to build it away from the ranch?" Jodie seemed incredulous at the thought.

"No," Marie admitted, "only—"

"Do you like what you've seen of the plans?"

"Tell the truth, we haven't looked at 'em. At least *I* haven't. I just can't bring myself to. I told her we don't want it."

"I'm surprised she didn't work things out to where you'd think building the house was your idea. That's the way she usually operates." Jodie paused to consider. "You know, she said something earlier when Tate left. She told him to be careful. She's never done that before. And when you put it together with— She's never had John Fellows visit the ranch before, either, has she? When she's used him in the past, she's always gone to his office. At least, as far as I know.''

''He's not been here that I know of. But maybe—'' The housekeeper tipped her head toward Claire. ''Maybe it's because—''

''Has she been told not to travel?'' Jodie asked, picking up on Marie's unspoken suggestion.

''Not to my knowledge,'' Claire answered truthfully.

Claire had expected a continuation of hostilities from Jodie when she'd seen her drive up with her family. Jodie had been the person most upset that afternoon at Shannon's. But either Jodie had come to a few conclusions on her own, or she'd been bombarded by the opinions of the other Parker women. In any case, her anger at Claire seemed to have disappeared.

Jodie glanced over her shoulder toward the living room. ''I have to get back. Marie, would you mind if I left Megan with you?''

''Heavens, no!'' Marie exclaimed, glancing at the little girl still at play on the floor. ''Lunch is just about ready, and I can't think of anythin' I'd like more than some time with my favorite little sweetheart.''

"*All* the Parker babies are your favorites," Jodie teased.

"You were my favorite, too...once," Marie bandied back.

"*Once?*" Jodie grinned as she straightened from chucking her daughter under the chin. "You mean I'm not now?"

"Mrie, play Megan," the toddler demanded as her mother turned to leave.

With some stiffness, Marie curled her legs under her and settled on the floor.

A stack of thin crustless sandwiches, cut into triangles, were arranged on a plate and partially covered with plastic wrap. Claire motioned to them and asked, "Is it all right if I take a couple of these with me for lunch? I thought I might go for a short walk."

"It's all right with me," Marie said. She started to get up again, but grimaced. "Could you finish coverin' 'em and put 'em in the refrigerator when you're done? That's what I was doin' when you folks came in. Now I'm down here—" she indicated her position on the floor with humor "—I don't know how I'm gonna get up. 'Mrie' couldn't refuse such a sweet little thing like you, though, could she?" She laughed and held her arms wide for the child to cuddle.

Claire chose her sandwich, then slipped the plate into the refrigerator.

"Get a drink or somethin', too," Marie urged. "And one of those salads. I made one for you."

"Thank you," Claire said.

"You already make arrangements about this with Miss Parker?"

"No."

"I'll tell her you wanted a little time on your own. She'll understand. There's a nice spot to eat out behind the barn. It's shaded this time a' day."

"Thank you," Claire repeated.

She carried her sandwich and salad outside, with a can of soda in her dress pocket.

A footpath led away from the main house, an alternate route to the work area and barn. Undoubtedly it was the path Axel used to go to work. Claire followed it now.

Mae had enough Parkers around her at present to look after her.

Also, Claire definitely didn't want to be in the same room with Tanner again so soon...even if they weren't alone.

"SO THIS IS WHERE YOU BOTH got off to," Jodie teased as she entered the ranch office and caught Rafe and Tanner setting up the new computer. "I had a feeling something was up."

Rafe sent her a sharp look. "Not a word," he ordered, and Jodie grinned.

"Of course not!" she vowed, and came closer to study the components Tanner had removed from the shipping box. "Wow...look at the size of that monitor. It's a lot bigger than the one I used in college. And the one Shannon uses, too. Not to mention the added factor that Aunt Mae doesn't know about it."

Rafe handed Tanner the cord he asked for. "All Aunt Mae needs is to see how it works. Tanner's going to show her."

Tanner straightened from linking the monitor and the computer. "*And* try to explain how it works. Backed up properly, no information should go missing."

"Good luck," Jodie said doubtfully.

"All set," Tanner announced as he moved around to the front of the desk. He glanced at his stepbrother, then at Jodie. "You want to give it the inaugural touch, Jodie? Press that button over there."

"This one?" Jodie asked, reaching for the tower, then she chortled as the video screen came to life.

"That's fine!" Rafe proclaimed proudly.

"What happens next?" Jodie asked.

"We need to see what program your neighbor is running, Rafe. The one you said you liked."

Rafe pulled a plastic shopping bag out of a drawer in the old file cabinet. "Already got it. Up in Fort Stockton. They have a big store full of this stuff."

"You went yourself?" Tanner asked.

"Sure did. Wanted to see what this new world was like. Sure is confusin'. The salesman asked me about my operating system and how big my hard drive is. Almost hit him for bein' nosy, not to mention personal."

Jodie and Tanner dissolved into laughter as Rafe had intended.

"You need to get off this ranch more, Rafe," Jodie said, trying to recover.

"Nothing wrong with this ranch."

"When do you want me to get started?" Tanner asked.

"Soon as you can. How's that arm?"

"What arm?" Tanner returned facetiously.

Rafe nodded and eyed Jodie. "What was goin' on up at the house when you left?"

"Aunt Mae said she wanted to rest. Sent us over to Harriet's. Aren't you worried she'll come down here and see this?"

Rafe shook his head. "She hasn't been down here in at least a month."

"That long?" Jodie breathed.

"She rarely leaves the house now. She'll sit out on the porch sometimes, but that's it."

Jodie's face had lost all animation. "I'm not liking this, Rafe."

"Neither am I," he returned grimly, "but what can we do?"

Jodie ran a finger along the base of the keyboard, careful not to depress any keys. "Have you noticed her doing anything a little...odd at times? She told Tate to be careful when he left earlier...seemed almost worried. That's not like her. She wouldn't want to worry me. And Marie told me she's had some plans drawn up for them...for a house."

Rafe's expression darkened. Tanner knew it had nothing to do with his great-aunt's generosity and everything to do with the reason behind it.

"John Fellows came to the ranch to see her today, too," Jodie added. "I saw him as Tate and I drove in. And she confirmed it."

"What's she up to now?" Rafe asked sharply.

"Checking up on Lurleen."

Rafe raked a hand through his hair. "Well, I guess we should be glad she's at least doin' something."

"But it's like—" Jodie stopped, bit her bottom lip. When Rafe's dark eyes lingered on hers, she continued, "It's like she thinks she doesn't have very long. Has she said anything unusual to you?"

There was a short silence before Rafe answered, "Nothin' she meant."

"What did she say?" Jodie demanded.

"That one day I'd be in charge, then I could do what I wanted. But she was mad about me wantin' Tanner to do the records."

"About a week ago, out of the blue, she called to tell me Tate and I should have another baby."

Rafe laughed shortly. "That's not unusual. She's pestered most of us about that over the years."

"It was the *way* she said it. Kind of wistful. Like she wouldn't be here when—" Once again, she had to stop her bottom lip from trembling.

"Maybe we're readin' too much into all this," Rafe said, wrapping an arm around her shoulders and giving her a bracing hug. He looked at Tanner. "You're an outsider. What do you think?"

"I mostly remember her from when I was a boy."

The two cousins waited for him to go on.

Tanner sighed. He wasn't going to get off so easily. "She's getting older. There's no denying it. But as to whether you're seeing things that aren't there—" He shrugged. "I couldn't say."

"You think maybe that little nurse would tell

you more than she's willin' to tell us?'' Rafe asked.

Tanner saw where this was heading. ''Have you tried talking to Mae's doctor?''

''He won't say a word,'' Rafe replied. ''Other than that she's doin' as good as can be expected. But I don't think passin' out is to be expected. Shannon's mentioned a pacemaker. You know anything about them?''

''I've wondered about that, too,'' Jodie agreed.

The intensity of their gazes was difficult to withstand. They wanted him to say he'd quiz Claire.

He made one last attempt. ''I don't know what good it'll do.''

''It'll give you another reason to talk with her,'' Rafe said dryly.

''I don't need your help with that, Rafe.''

'''Scuse me,'' Rafe bandied back, then jostled Jodie's elbow. ''Somebody sure got sensitive all of a sudden.''

''Please, Tanner?'' Jodie pleaded, not as ready as Rafe to release the pressure.

Tanner nodded his assent, and he knew when he made the commitment that he'd probably regret it.

Claire was… Claire was different. Earlier, when they were in the bathroom, it would have been so easy to shut the door and— The problem was, she was too much like the skittish foal he'd watched

Rafe rescue that morning. Even though the young horse had a bad gash in her front leg, she had all the wild instincts of the herd she'd become separated from. She'd refused to let Rafe get near her. They'd had to chase her into a box canyon to have even half a chance, and then only his stepbrother's deft horsemanship and roping ability had allowed her capture.

Claire seemed equally skittish.

She wasn't about to go near a box canyon, and his roping skills were abysmal. If he started to ask questions…

Jodie hugged him. And behind her, Rafe sanctioned his capitulation with a raised thumb.

Tanner wasn't nearly as sure of his success as they were.

CHAPTER TEN

"YOU ENJOY EATIN' YOUR lunch outside?" Mae growled when Claire returned to the house. She'd caught up with the matriarch in the hall, on her way to the bedroom.

Mae looked tired. Her shoulders drooped, her cane tapped at a slower pace.

"Yes, very much," Claire said. She surreptitiously wrapped an arm around the elderly woman's waist. Mae hadn't needed this level of support since the day of her arrival.

At Claire's touch, Mae stiffened, then relaxed. "I'd've appreciated hearin' direct from you. Next time, say somethin'!"

"It was an impulse. Your family was here, and I thought you might like a little time alone with them. They accept me now. You don't have to keep pushing me at them."

"What do you mean?" Mae shot her a narrowed look.

"You've been trying to accustom them to me. Well, it's worked. They're being very nice."

"Even Jodie?" she demanded, dropping the pretense.

"Even Jodie," Claire confirmed.

Mae was compliant as Claire assisted her into a light dressing gown and helped her into bed. Her eyes followed Claire's every move as she hung up her clothes and performed a quick check of the bedside table. Only when she started to leave did Mae protest.

"No, don't go," she said.

The disquiet in the woman's tone stopped Claire more than her actual words.

"May I do something for you?" she asked.

"I don't want you to leave." Mae motioned her to the chair.

"Are you feeling faint?" Claire asked, moving closer.

"No."

"Something else?"

"No."

Claire wrinkled her brow. "Do you want me to call the doctor? Or check your vital signs myself?"

"*No.*"

"Then what—"

"I don't want to be alone."

Fear was an emotion Claire would never have associated with Mae Parker, but its presence proved her human. The woman needed a distraction so she wouldn't have to listen to her own thoughts.

As she settled in the chair, Claire glanced at the book on the bedside table. "Would you like me to read to you?" she asked.

"Talk to me. Tell me about yourself."

"Miss Parker—"

"*Mae,*" Mae corrected her yet again.

Claire sighed to herself. The woman was nothing if not determined.

"Do you want to know how I came into nursing?" she asked.

"Eventually, yes, but start further back. At the beginning."

Claire had prepared a stripped-down version of her life for just such an occasion. "I was born in South Texas, in Corpus Christi. I grew up there, graduated from high school there. A few years after that I moved to Austin. Then I ended up in Midland."

"You're leavin' a lot out," Mae complained.

"My life isn't very exciting," Claire replied lightly.

"Do you want me to put John Fellows on your trail?"

Claire didn't know whether to be amused or taken aback. "You wouldn't do something like that."

"Wanna try me?"

The woman's eyelids drooped as she issued the challenge, signaling Claire that if she danced around with vague truths a little longer, the matriarch would soon be asleep.

"I grew up in and around Corpus Christi, made good grades. I was in a play once in high school, but I didn't like being on stage. I could never remember the lines. Someone was always having to prompt me. And with all those people watching—"

Claire let her words peter out. Mae had grown very still. After several minutes, she stood up.

The dark eyes opened instantly. "What about your family?" the woman demanded. "You might as well tell me, because I mean to know."

"I don't understand why you think my life is so interesting."

"Tell me," Mae insisted.

Talking about herself went against Claire's primary rule. Yet, at the same time, Mae Parker had the means to cut through any bureaucratic red tape. She could find out on her own.

"Someone found me on the hood of a junked car in an alleyway when I was about two days old. The authorities took me away, found homes for me...and I'm here."

Mae was silent. Finally, she barked out, "You weren't adopted?"

"No."

"You said 'homes.' How many were there?"

"A few."

"How many's a few?"

"I lost count." Claire lifted her gaze. "Miss Parker— Mae, I truly don't—"

"So you've never had a real family," Mae concluded. "What about someone you were close to? There had to be a person like that, didn't there? At some point in time?"

"Yes."

"Well, whoever it was should be commended. Was it a woman? What was her name?"

Claire wanted the interrogation to end. She didn't want to specify Mrs. Stanton's name or talk about the role the woman had played in her young life. Nor did she want to divulge how, when each time she'd start to think of somewhere as home, something would happen—a foster parent would fall ill, there would be trouble in the marriage, social services would experience some kind of organizational hiccup.

"I'm not comfortable talking about it," she said. "So, if you don't mind—"

"I *knew* there was somethin' different about you. Not in a bad way. Somethin' good."

Claire started to move away, but Mae again stopped her retreat.

"I'm not done yet. Now it's my turn to tell you somethin' *I* don't like talkin' about."

The elderly woman pushed herself up to lean against her pillow. When Claire automatically came to fluff it, Mae almost as automatically snapped, "No, don't."

As she resettled in the chair, Claire was half curious and half dreading what would follow.

"I'm worried that I'm not gonna be brave about all this," Mae stated simply. "About what's comin'. You've probably had a good talk with Dr. Stevens by now and he's told you everything. That's why I'm in such a hurry to get the family all worked out. I figure if I do, when I get up there—" she jerked a thumb heavenward "—the others won't be so hard on me for not doin' a good enough job."

"What others?" Claire asked.

"Gibson and Virgil and my daddy and—"

"I don't see how they could possibly think you haven't done a good job. From what I've heard—"

Mae waved a hand impatiently. "Aw, I've made a mess of a lot of things. I told you about Gib. Then there's Richard—Darlene and Thomas's son. Those two are off on one of their trips right now, so you haven't met 'em. They're always off on a trip these days. Well, Richard and Ann got a divorce. If I just coulda got in on it earlier I might've been able to stop it, but I didn't know until it was already too late. Then there's Gloria—Rafe's mom and Tanner's stepmom. I shoulda patched things up with her a long time ago. Not been so proud and so stubborn. And most important, Rafe. I'm not sure I've given over to him enough. He runs the ranch fine, but I don't know if I've got him believin' he can take over the family and look after things like he should. I've known I've needed to, but— I just couldn't let go! I've said things, done things that've probably made everythin' worse.''

Moisture had gathered in Mae's dark eyes as she spoke. Claire reached for her hand, and it fluttered lightly in her grasp.

''Most times I'm fine,'' Mae said huskily. ''But just now...seein' Jodie...'' She was unable to go on.

''You're wondering if it could be for the last time,'' Claire stated for her.

Mae nodded.

''Will she leave today without saying goodbye?'' Claire asked quietly.

''No.''

''Then it wasn't for the last time, was it? You'll see her again in a little while.''

Mae considered the gentle logic, then, she, too,

smiled. "I guess I never thought of it that way. And I'll see her tomorrow, too—at the barbecue, along with everyone else."

Claire had heard nothing about a barbecue, but she was far down the list of people to be told of these things. "Yes," she said.

Loosening her hand, Mae took a swipe at her damp lashes. "A family barbecue will mean you'll be meetin' a lot more people," she warned. "Are you up to that?"

"I'm a lot tougher than I look," Claire claimed, taking her cue from the woman's lifting spirits.

Mae smiled at her small jest, but said seriously, "I'm comin' to think you are. Now, let me get some rest. I want to play with little Megan when she and Jodie come back from visitin' Harriet."

As Claire left the room, the matriarch settled herself contentedly for her nap.

A SMALL GLASS FISH, a plastic bunny pin, a photo of a tree house, a hand-carved brass dog…

Claire's fingers moved from keepsake to keepsake. The collection on the bedcover would mean little to anyone else. To her, it meant the world. Each item came with a memory that anchored her to a place and time. From her fifth birthday on she'd tried to find something to take with her from each place she stayed. They were *her* history.

The Parkers had theirs; she had hers.

She had nothing from the Fitzgeralds, though. She hadn't thought she would need anything; then when it all went terribly wrong and she'd left the house so abruptly, she'd been in too much emotional pain to search for remembrances.

What would she take from this place? she wondered. Something to remind her of the ranch, but insignificant enough that no one would object.

Restlessly she moved from the bed. She couldn't let herself be drawn into these people's lives. Not Mae's, not anyone's.

She'd responded to Mae's admission of fear as she would to any patient, trying to get her to see that each moment was precious. That dwelling on the uncertain future wasted precious time.

Claire distracted herself from her own thoughts by returning the collection to its drawer inside the wardrobe trunk. Then she took her notebook, curled into her chair and tried to reproduce the intricate leaves and flowers of the potted geranium someone had placed on her small table.

TANNER AND RAFE RETURNED to the compound in the early evening. The afternoon had gone well. Tanner had installed the software program Rafe had purchased and adjusted it to his stepbrother's needs. Then, as he began to input information from the records, he started teaching Rafe how to use the system. Rafe had never touched a computer before, so the process had been tedious. Rafe was determined to learn, though. And Tanner appreciated his stepbrother's tenacity as well as his sense of humor.

"Mae's gonna love it, if she ever gives it a chance," Rafe said enthusiastically. "Now, with me runnin' it—" He laughed in self-deprecation. "Maybe we'd better not break that bit of news to her at the same time we tell her what we've done. 'Cause then she'll be positive the ranch is goin' to hell!"

"You're doing fine," Tanner assured him. "Just as you told me about ranch work, you can't expect to learn everything in one day. That goes for computers, too."

Rafe grinned. "Shannon'll sure want one of these new ones as soon as she sees it. Expect a visit from her in the office tomorrow."

They parted ways at the head of the gravel drive—Rafe going on to his home and Tanner heading into the main house.

Since he and Rafe had bummed thick roast beef sandwiches from Axel an hour earlier, Tanner decided to stop by the kitchen to tell Marie not to bother with dinner for him. He found Jodie and the housekeeper in a goodbye hug.

Both women looked tense as they separated, and Tanner had no trouble identifying the cause—Mae.

"Oh! You're back early," Marie said, slightly flustered. She glanced at the clock. "Oh, my heavens, it's later than I thought! But never mind, I can fix you somethin' in two seconds flat."

"I've eaten," Tanner said, smiling easily. "That's what I was coming to tell you. Hi, Jodie."

Jodie's eyes twinkled at him. "Long time no see, Tanner," she drawled humorously.

"Yeah," Tanner returned. "Long time."

Jodie had hung around the office until he had the program up and going, but when he began to explain to Rafe the rudiments of elementary mousing principles, she left. "*This* I don't want to see," she'd quipped, and, chuckling, abandoned them to their efforts.

"You, uh, have a good afternoon?" she inquired drolly.

"Fair. We're progressing."

Marie, who had no clue that they weren't discussing his efforts to learn ranch work, chimed in, "I've heard you're gettin' better with a rope."

Tanner laughed. "Well, I did manage to catch what I aimed at this morning. But since it was standing still—"

"What was it?" Jodie challenged.

"A fence post."

She grinned. "The one with the barbed wire that got you?"

"Jodie!" Marie reproved.

With mock seriousness Tanner answered, "I was wholly innocent of assaulting that particular post. This was another one."

"I may have to tell Tate," Jodie teased. "And if I do, he'll probably want to have a little talk with you tomorrow. Can't have you goin' around assaultin' innocent Parker fence posts. That is—" she lost her smile "—if he can come tomorrow."

"Miss Mae wants everybody out for a barbecue," Marie informed Tanner, then glanced at Jodie. "That's what we were talkin' about just now. She only told us about it late this afternoon. Usually, she gives us a lot more warnin'. But not this time." The housekeeper shook her head with worry.

Tension, again, overtook the two women.

"It's not like her to put so much work on Axel and Marie without notice," Jodie said. "They have so much to prepare. Not to mention the rest of us. I'm supposed to be at a meeting at Emma's tomorrow. And Tate...I don't know if he can get away. But Aunt Mae says she wants *all* of us to be here."

"She wants Jim Cleary, too. And Jack Denton," Marie said.

"I'm supposed to call Jack when I get home," Jodie added in agreement. "You remember Jack, don't you, Tanner? He was the sheriff in Briggs County before Tate?"

"Vaguely," Tanner replied.

Jodie hesitated a second, as if wondering if more discussion would help in any way, then she sighed. "I guess I'd better go get Megan away from Dad. Otherwise, he'll have started another painting. Did he show either of you the one with her and Gene? It's wonderful."

She hugged Marie again, then lightheartedly hugged Tanner, before she left the house by the back door.

Marie turned to Tanner. "You sure you don't want somethin' to eat?" she asked.

"No, I'm fine," Tanner said. "Where is everyone?"

"Miss Mae's gone to her room, and Claire—I feel funny callin' her Claire since I was so grouchy to her at first—I'm not sure where she is. Probably with Miss Mae."

Tanner glanced around the kitchen. "I'm not much of a cook, but if you or Axel need any help—"

"Axel could probably use some help settin' up

tables and such tomorrow mornin' in the courtyard, after he starts the briskets cookin'.''

"Tell him I'll be there," Tanner said. And, warmed by the housekeeper's approval, he went upstairs.

CLAIRE DID HER BEST TO stay quiet in the parlor after Mae chose an early night. She read more of the family history, but couldn't settle into it for long. Drawing didn't satisfy her. Neither did the books on the shelves.

Rarely did she have such a hard time finding something to occupy herself. Possibly she, too, was tired from the day. Jodie and Megan had returned to the main house after Mae's rest, accompanied by Harriet, Shannon and little Nikki. The two toddlers were only a month apart and they played well together, but it was hardly relaxing with the mothers constantly up and down and the noise from the excited children.

Mae had been amazingly tolerant of it all, according to Harriet's aside. Claire, privy to the reason behind the matriarch's apparent mellowness, only nodded.

The full group of visitors hadn't stayed long. Harriet and Shannon returned to their homes, and Mae had then claimed her playtime with the little redhead.

Claire had not been allowed to leave, once again at Mae's determined insistence. Several times she'd caught the elderly woman watching her, and knew it was because of what she'd told her about her childhood.

Once again Claire made a restive circuit of the parlor. She couldn't sleep when it was still light and she didn't want to lie in bed waiting for darkness. Too much had happened that day. Too much she didn't want to have boomerang back.

She checked Mae, saw that she was fast asleep, then let herself soundlessly into the hall. Since she'd arrived, she had yet to see a sunset here. A sunset would be her reward for this long and difficult day. She'd find a chair, tote it onto the balcony and take pleasure in one of nature's natural beauties.

Claire saw no one as she mounted the stairs to the second floor, or as she made her way into the bedroom. She went straight to the French doors and stepped to the balcony railing.

"Ah!" she murmured in delight at her perfect timing. The cloud-streaked sky boasted an amazing array of colors—pinks, blues, golds, violets.

"Kinda nice, huh…as Rafe would say."

Tanner's husky voice shattered her short-lived enjoyment. She whirled to face him.

He sat with his long jeans-clad legs outstretched and crossed at the ankle.

"What are you doing here?" she demanded. She'd thought he was still with Rafe, doing whatever it was Rafe had wanted him to do.

He smiled slowly. "I'm contemplating nature...and life. My life."

A way out. "I'll leave you to it, then," she said, and turned to bolt back into the house.

He glanced at the ample space along her side of the balcony. "Plenty of room here for two. And the show's free. It's really been nice."

Claire glanced over her shoulder at the sunset, then back at him. "I don't want to intrude."

"If you were intruding, I'd tell you."

Her alternative was to return to the parlor and effectively be trapped. She found a chair in the bedroom, brought it outside and sat down after pointedly placing it a good distance from his.

"I forgot," he said, sitting up. "You don't like *your* plans disrupted. I'll leave. I've been here long enough to have my fill."

Claire frowned to herself. She couldn't let him do that. "No," she replied. "It's all right. You can stay."

She tried to ignore him as he once again extended his legs, recrossed his boots and heaved a sigh of contentment. Minutes later she broke the silence, so as not to be considered totally antisocial. "Mae went to bed early tonight."

"I figured that."

"I just thought—in case you wondered."

"Why would I wonder?"

The colors across the western sky altered, some fading, some intensifying.

She tried again. "Your boots…they don't look new anymore."

He lifted one to examine it. "Nope."

"Mae would consider that a plus."

"Mae would consider a missing fingertip a plus." At her startled look, he explained. "Happens sometimes if a cowboy's not careful. He throws out his rope to catch a cow or steer and part of his finger can get sliced off if it's in the wrong place when the rope pulls taut. The man who's teaching me is missing the tips of two fingers on his right hand."

"Surely you don't think Mae would want something like that to happen to you."

"Not want it, no. But if it did, she'd consider it part of the job."

"But it's not your real job. Not what you do."

"It's what I'm doing now." He chuckled lightly. "Although I have a way to go before I'm in much danger. First, you have to be able to catch a moving cow."

Claire had never thought of a cowboy's work as dangerous.

"If you could do it, would you take the chance?" she asked.

"I would."

"Why?"

"Because I'd like to show myself I could. And show Rafe."

The sky colors had darkened into deeper hues—more blue, more purple and deep pink—as the sun dipped lower behind the distant mountains.

"What about you?" he asked. "If you wanted to prove something to yourself, wouldn't you do it?"

"I don't have anything to prove."

He cocked his head. "There's never been something that makes you wonder if what you're doing with your time is worthwhile?"

"What I do *is* worthwhile."

"Then why aren't you happy doing it?"

The presumptuousness of his retort rattled her. "I'm happy," she claimed.

"Are you? Then why don't you smile more often?"

Again, questions. Claire got to her feet and headed for the bedroom, but Tanner quickly inserted himself in the doorway.

"Look, I'm sorry. That was completely out of line. I didn't have the right to say what I did."

"I smile," Claire insisted in her own defense.

"You haven't smiled more than once or twice in the week you've been here."

"You haven't been in the house all the time."

"Are you telling me you smile when I'm not around?"

Claire had a hard time keeping up. He was saying things—serious things—yet at the same time, he was smiling. And she—

The magnetic pull she'd felt before increased, until her insides twisted in a way that frightened her.

She tried to make her legs work. She had to get away from here. From him.

His smile flickered, then disappeared as he took a step closer and touched her cheek in a feather-light caress.

She heard his short intake of breath.

Then, in the next second, his mouth lowered to cover hers.

CHAPTER ELEVEN

CLAIRE MELTED UNDER THE high-voltage intensity of Tanner's kiss. All thought, all perspective were lost to her. All she could do was feel. She stood on tiptoe, straining to meet his embrace.

His mouth lit fires inside her, made her curl her fingers into his hard-muscled shoulders, made her press herself against him. Made her moan in pleasure as he trailed his lips down her neck to the hollow between her breasts.

Yet when he tugged on the fastener to the front zip of her dress, reality returned with a hard thump.

She pushed him away, then pushed harder when he didn't seem to understand.

"Claire—" He murmured her name.

She stepped back, both hands shielding the fastener.

How had that happened? They'd been standing and talking, then— How could she have let those next few seconds get so far out of hand? How could she have so quickly and easily thrown over years of rigid self-discipline?

She remembered where they stood—in full view of anyone who might pass by the main house.

"I could be fired for this," she whispered unevenly.

"This isn't the nineteenth century."

"I could still be fired."

"It won't happen."

A tremor passed over her. She glanced at the open French doors. "I—I have to go," she said. She'd known they shouldn't be alone together.

"Claire—" He reached for her, but she evaded him.

"Just…let me go," she said as she hurried away—into the bedroom, down the stairs and back to the bedroom parlor.

Her heart beat as rapidly as a bird's as she curled onto the bed.

She'd set herself a path, and for all these years she'd followed it. She'd looked after her clients to the best of her ability, but didn't get involved with them. She'd dealt with the client's family—if they had a family—but never got involved with them, either.

She'd learned a hard lesson after humiliating herself so thoroughly with Bryan Fitzgerald. The pain and embarrassment had seared the folly of such a sentiment into her mind. She'd tried to cover her shock at the easy way Bryan had dismissed her, but she'd known she'd failed when she saw realization dawn in his eyes. The awkward moments that followed had hurt most of all.

Over the next difficult weeks, she'd developed two rules: Never again let yourself get close to anyone, and never let anyone get close to you.

A new client, a new home. Moving from place to place was easy for her. She'd been doing it her entire life.

What a person doesn't have…

Shadows lengthened in the room. Soon, she would be able to hide in the full darkness of night.

But would she be able to hide from herself?

TANNER STOOD IN THE gathering darkness, his fingers wrapped around the cool wrought-iron railing.

He hadn't meant to kiss her—not that she'd believe him. It had just…happened.

Everything inside him demanded that he seek her out. Make her listen. Make her—

He groaned as he remembered how it had felt when she'd responded.

What was happening to him?

He wasn't prepared for added complications in his life. He had to get his head straight. Deal with what had happened to Danny. Deal with his sense of guilt. Figure out what to do with the rest of his life.

The waxing moon grew in brilliance as night deepened. A cricket chirped, soon joined by another.

Tanner, hearing their calls, didn't move.

"I WANT A BARBECUE. Anything wrong with that?" Mae answered Rafe's puzzled query with aggression.

"Not a thing in the world, Aunt Mae," he said. "It's just such short notice, I'm not sure everyone will be able to—"

"They'll be here," the matriarch said confidently.

"But why today? Why not next—"

"Because I *feel* like havin' it today."

Mae tapped past Claire to the living room mantel, where she stopped in front of the painting of ranch headquarters and straightened it.

"Do you have an objection to us havin' a barbecue today?" she asked, turning back.

"We were plannin' to clean out a water tank this afternoon."

"You can do it another day, can't you?"

"Sure we can."

"Then do it. I don't ask for much, Rafe."

The outrageous claim seemed to flabbergast him, but after a moment he laughed. "No, you don't ask...you tell!"

Mae lifted her chin in place of a reply. She'd awakened that morning "full of spit and vinegar," she'd told Claire, with no sign of last night's lassitude.

"All right," Rafe agreed. "We'll put off cleaning the tank. If you want a barbecue, you've got a barbecue. And today's the day."

"Now tell me you won't enjoy it," Mae exhorted, meaning just the opposite.

"I always enjoy one of Axel and Marie's special meals."

"And seein' everybody?"

"And seein' everybody."

The man's high regard for his elderly great-aunt was palpable. He'd smiled through the ripostes and continued smiling until he noticed Claire watching him, then his good humor disappeared.

Rafe continued to be the last holdout in accepting Claire at the ranch. He no longer treated her with outright hostility, but his formal manner spoke for itself. It didn't surprise her that after giving his aunt a parting nod, he offered her a much briefer one on his way out.

"Rafe's a good man," Mae said gruffly as the front door closed. "The ranch and the family couldn't be in better hands."

Claire suffered an unexpected twinge at the elderly woman's oblique reference to her future passing. She quickly dispelled it.

"Come on, let's go find us some breakfast," Mae said, and they resumed their interrupted journey into the dining room.

As Claire settled the fine linen napkin on her lap, she wondered how she was going to eat anything. Her stomach had roiled since Mae awakened her that morning from a final fitful snatch of sleep. If she'd slept a complete hour in the night, she'd be surprised.

The kiss seemed a dream. But it wasn't. It had happened.

And it was inevitable she would see Tanner today.

She resolved to ignore him.

AT BREAKFAST AND DURING the hours that followed, Mae retreated into her own world. Plotting? Planning? Anticipating? Claire stayed near her side, glad for a short respite before what promised to be a difficult afternoon.

"We're goin' to have an interesting time," Mae said with satisfaction as she put the finishing touches to her barbecue attire shortly before noon. She looked crisp and dignified in a tan twill skirt and a white cotton blouse with a bright scarf accenting the neckline.

She studied Claire's reflection in the vanity table mirror and frowned. "You're not goin' to wear one of those uniform things today, are you?" she challenged. "This is a special day. I want you to look good."

Claire glanced down at her pastel blue dress. "I think this is about right. I'm not a guest, and I'd feel uncomfortable pretending to be one."

"You're *my* guest," Mae shot back. "At least, today you are."

"Mae...please," Claire appealed. "I truly feel better in this."

Mae's displeasure endured, but she bowed to Claire's wishes. "Sometime I'd like to see you in somethin' different. But if that's what you want to wear..."

"Thank you," Claire said.

It was extremely important that she preserve every vestige of her office. She *wasn't* a guest. She couldn't allow herself to be treated as one. She *had* to stay separate. Maintain her practiced detachment. That way, when her assignment ended, she could put her trunk back on the roof of her car and leave the ranch without so much as a—

Claire gave her head a tiny jerk. She wouldn't leave the ranch unless Mae— She didn't want to think about Mae dying!

Mae turned to face her. "What's the matter with

you?'' she demanded. "You sick or somethin'? You're twitchin'." She gestured to the foot of the bed. "Sit down for a minute. There's something I want to tell you."

Obeying, Claire perched on the corner of the cream satin cover.

"If you're worried about what you told me yesterday, you don't need to be. I take people as I find 'em, not for their pedigree. I like you, Claire Hannaford. I like what I see. You can't help what happened to you as a baby—what your mama and daddy did. All you can do is be responsible for who you are now. *What* you are now. Nothin' else matters."

Tears pricked at Claire's eyes. No one had ever sat her down and said something so supportive. She blinked the moisture away. Her value to her patients was the serenity she brought them. Her calmness, her composure.

"I—I've always believed that, too," she said.

The matriarch's gaze never wavered from her face. "Good," she said crisply. "Now, let's see how everything's settin' up. People should start arrivin' anytime now."

"SEE?" MAE SWEPT BACK THE sheer curtain in one of the long front windows of the living room. "Axel's been barbecuing since before dawn, and while it's cookin', he sets up the tables.'' She sniffed the wonderful aromas coming from the kitchen. ''And Marie's been cookin' ever since she got our breakfast out of the way. I love family get-togethers and havin' friends over.''

Claire saw two men arranging a number of wooden tables into several rows. One was Axel…the other, Tanner.

Another jolt of electricity shot through her at seeing him, but she held on to her resolve. From the way Mae's mouth had trembled at the mention of family and friends, she wasn't the only one having to exert strong discipline on herself. Mae was determined to savor this day.

Mae frowned as she continued to gaze out the window. ''Go tell Tanner to move all the tables to the left a little. There'll be too much sun later where they are.''

Claire blinked. She hadn't expected… ''You want me to—''

''Tell him to move 'em to the left a foot.'' Mae became more specific.

The last thing Claire wanted was contact with Tanner, yet she went to the front door, took a breath and stepped onto the porch. If she could get away with shouting Mae's instruction from there, she would, but she knew she couldn't. She descended the steps and crossed the gravel drive.

Axel looked up as she drew nearer and nudged Tanner's arm. Tanner stopped what he was doing.

"Mae wants you to move the tables to the left a foot," Claire said, addressing Axel.

"She what?" Axel asked, clearly puzzled.

"Mae…move the tables to the left…about a foot. Something to do with too much sun later where they are now."

Axel scratched his bald head. "This is always where I put 'em."

"I'm only the messenger," Claire said with a shrug.

"'Mornin', Claire," Tanner drawled in a good imitation of the usual ranch greeting.

"Good morning," she murmured, determined not to look at him for more than a second. His husky voice saying her name again and that smile hinting at a shared secret knowledge were more than she felt able to deal with right then. She hadn't been prepared to see him so soon.

Axel heaved a sigh. "Well," he said, "I guess if that's what she wants us to do, we'd better do it." He reached for the end of the outside table and waited for Tanner to heft the other end.

Claire used that moment to escape back into the house.

She didn't realize how revealing her expression must have been until Mae remarked, "What's up

with you? You look like you just went a round
with a bobcat, and the bobcat won! You and Tanner have a problem? You didn't seem particularly
friendly to him out there.''

Claire cast about for something to say. ''No,
nothing's wrong. I'm trying to remember if I
needed to call the agency yesterday. I'll call them
on Monday…just to be sure.''

Mae turned again to look out the window, but
Claire sensed she didn't believe her.

A HALF HOUR LATER THE wood plank tables had
been covered with white cloths and all the needed
accoutrements, and family and friends had started
to arrive.

''Used to be, eight or ten years back,'' Mae told
Claire as they stood in the courtyard, ''we could
all fit at one a' these tables. Now we've grown
so— Morgan!'' She interrupted herself to call to a
blond man of about the same age and build as
Rafe. ''Come meet Claire.''

Pale blue eyes in a handsome sun-bronzed face
smiled at Claire. ''I've heard about you from both
Rafe and Christine.''

''And Christine—'' Mae included the pretty
brunette Claire had met at Shannon's house.

''We've met,'' Christine said, and embraced her
lightly.

A little girl of about four with a mass of curly blond hair held hands with a young woman in her late teens or early twenties. The young woman could be mistaken for no one but a Parker. She had glossy black hair, huge dark eyes and a serious face.

Christine brought the two forward. "Claire, these are our daughters, Erin and Beth." She introduced the older daughter first.

"Nice to meet you," Erin said quietly.

Claire liked her right away, sensing a similar reticence to her own.

"And Dub and Delores Hughes, Morgan's parents," Mae continued, bringing others forward. "Dub used to be the ranch foreman before Morgan took over."

"Nice to meet ya," Dub said, repeating Erin's greeting.

Delores smiled and took her hand.

The older Hugheses were in their seventies, both easily seen to be salt-of-the-earth types. Friendly as well as curious.

"Are Quint and Katlin gonna make it in?" Mae demanded, shooting a glance at Morgan.

"I drove out and told 'em myself yesterday afternoon, soon as I heard. They said they'd be here."

Mae smiled approval. "Good. Glad to hear it.

Quint is Delores's nephew," Mae told Claire. "He and Katlin live out in Big Spur Division. Long way from here. Takes a while to get from place to place."

Claire vaguely remembered having heard those names her first evening at the ranch.

"Emma!" Mae turned to greet someone else. "Jack!"

Claire was soon introduced to a slim middle-aged woman with a short silver wedge who seemed a little disconcerted by Mae's enthusiasm. Emma Connelly, Claire was reminded, was Tate Connelly's mother.

Jack turned out to be a large man, well up in his sixties, who still looked powerful though he sported a comfortable belly roll. His thinning silver curls grew close to his head, and his brown eyes, only a shade darker than his skin, danced with friendly interest as he met Claire.

"Jack Denton was sheriff of Briggs County for over forty years, Claire," Mae explained. "Then he decided to let Tate take over for him."

"I did that twice," Jack quipped cheerfully. "Had him, lost him, then got him back again."

Tate came up behind the old sheriff and slapped a hand on his shoulder. "Whatcha sayin', Jack? Somethin' I should know?"

"Na, nothin' special. Just fillin' Claire in a little."

"Don't believe everything he says," Tate confided, grinning as he poked fun.

The men were longtime friends, Claire could see. And the fact that Jodie had become less suspicious made a difference in the lawman's bearing toward her. He didn't look so much like a lawman today, though, dressed in black jeans and a pale yellow shirt.

"Mi-Mae!" Megan squealed, straining against Jodie's hold. She reached for a kiss from her great-great-aunt, and laughingly, Jodie facilitated the event.

LeRoy and Harriet's family joined the group and hugs were given all around. About the same time Shannon, Rafe and their children swelled the ranks and more hugs and laughter ensued. Then Gib showed up, completing the roll call of ranch Parkers.

Marie delivered pitchers of iced tea and cold water from the main house to the table set off to one side for serving. People helped themselves as they broke into smaller groups, some standing, some sitting in scattered chairs.

Claire did her best to remain apart, even as she stayed within calling distance of Mae.

The matriarch's cheerfulness and buoyancy

seemed to take more than Emma Connelly by surprise. Claire sensed the family wasn't sure whether to enjoy the phenomenon or to be worried by it. But her high spirits were infectious and those around her soon relaxed.

Claire was introduced to the next batch of arrivals.

Quint McCabe was another long, lean blond cowboy-type with pale blue eyes and bronzed skin. He looked enough like Morgan Hughes to be his younger brother instead of his cousin. At Quint's side was a pretty young brunette named Katlin Brown. They'd alighted from a dusty green ranch pickup, and one was seldom more than two feet from the other. An older barrel-chested man joined the group.

"Jim Cleary is our nearest neighbor and great friend," Mae said. "Jim, my nurse, Claire Hannaford."

The curious look in the man's bright blue eyes told Claire that he'd heard of her as well. Did the whole county know about her? she wondered. But then, the Parkers had a large influence in the area. It was only natural that the latest neighborly goings-on would make for rampant gossip on the isolated ranches.

"Okay, does that mean everyone's here?" Rafe raised his voice as he bounced his little girl on his knee. At a shouted affirmative, he called out, "All right! Let's get the grub on then!"

His older son ran to give the word to Axel and Marie.

Claire had noted an absence, but no one else seemed to think it significant. She understood why when Axel brought the slabs of charred brisket from the cook house. Tanner came with him, helping to carry the large pan.

A good-hearted cheer went up in the courtyard.

Marie, assisted by the older girls, ferried steaming bowls and platters from the kitchen. All were placed along the serving table, with Axel's brisket given place of honor at the head.

"Looks as good as usual, Axel," Morgan Hughes called. "Who's your new helper? Get tired of doin' ranch work, Tanner? Decide you'd rather be assistant camp cook?"

"It has its advantages," Tanner called back, and helped himself to a blackened strip of meat that had come away from the rest.

Axel stabbed a sharp-pronged fork into one of the charred chunks and began to carve juicy slices with a wickedly sharp knife. "Takes a real man to be a cook," he declared.

"'Course, it does." Dub laughed. "We all agree. 'Specially when you got one a' them carvin' instruments in your hand."

"Darn tootin'," Axel shot back.

Everyone laughed and formed an informal line to help themselves to the bounty. Mae was in the lead.

A substantial chair waited at the head of the first table—for Mae's use when she finished the line. But once she filled her plate, instead of taking that place, she chose the seat next to it at the end of the bench. When Rafe approached, plate in hand, she directed him to the chair.

"No, Aunt Mae. That's your place," Rafe said.

Mae held her head high. "No, it's yours now."

Everyone stopped what they were doing, some still in line, others finding places along the benches.

"Aunt Mae—" Rafe protested.

"Don't argue, boy, I want you to have it. Why make everything such a battle? You're due it. Take it."

Rafe looked around at the others, abashed at the turn of events.

The significance of Mae's action was not lost on anyone there, even to Claire.

Encouraging smiles urged Rafe to do as Mae wished.

He came forward slowly to claim the seat, his lips tight, his jaw clamped.

The others resumed what they were doing. As

did Claire. She'd waited purposefully to go back for her own plate until she'd seen Mae seated. Mae hadn't liked it, but again Claire insisted.

The food smelled wonderful. Cooked carrots, fresh green beans, mounds of potato salad, coleslaw, heated squares of corn bread, a thick chili sauce, green chili peppers.

She helped herself to small bits of most things. But only when she drew near the head of the serving table did she wish that she could speed through. The last time she'd seen Tanner, he'd been helping Axel. Yet as she peered ahead to where the older man still worked, Tanner was nowhere in sight.

"The Parkers really know how to put on a spread, don't they?" he asked from directly behind her. Without her knowledge, he'd slipped into line behind her. His plate was heaped.

"Yes, they do," she replied coolly, although *cool* was not at all what she felt.

Axel grinned and gave her a slice of beef that covered half her plate.

"Oh, that's too much!" she cried.

"Wait'll you taste it," Tanner advised.

"You'll be comin' back for seconds," Axel teased.

When they moved away from the serving line,

only two places remained at the tables—both side by side at the end of the far table.

Claire moved past one of the two high chairs used by the younger children and claimed the seat across from Shannon, catercorner to the old sheriff.

Shannon looked up from an unsuccessful attempt to get her young daughter to eat a green bean.

"Nikki's into carrots now," she said ruefully. "She's at that age. But I guess it's better than Ward's potato chip fixation and Nate's ice cream. It's a wonder those two boys survived." When Tanner eased into place beside Claire, Shannon noted his loaded plate and teased, "Then, again, boys do tend to make up for any loss of vitamins once they grow up."

Tanner made no apologies. He adjusted the two giant slices of beef that Axel had placed on top the rest of his meal and quipped, "Darned hard smelling this meat cook all morning and not be ready to eat when it's time." He flashed a smile. "Axel is some cook!"

"That's why Rafe never has a hard time finding extra hands for the roundups," Shannon said. "As long as Axel's cooking, they'll be here. Marie's pretty good, too."

The close quarters along the wooden bench caused Claire to feel Tanner's every move. Their elbows brushed, their thighs touched. She could even smell the smoke on his hair and clothes from his morning in the cook house.

To help keep her mind on her duty, she glanced at Mae to see how she was doing and found that the matriarch continued to enjoy herself. But as she watched her, Mae looked over her shoulder several times—toward the end of the U-shaped drive where the narrow road led to and from the ranch. Was she expecting someone else? Claire wondered. Rafe had seemed to think everyone was here.

"Aren't you hungry?" Tanner asked. He spoke softly, only to her.

She shook her head.

There was a long pause, then, equally softly, he said, "About last night—"

Jodie's voice cut into his words. "Who's that?" she demanded from her seat halfway down the center table. She looked past everyone to the road.

A late-model maroon sedan turned into the far arm of the U-shaped drive.

Unlike the others, Claire didn't continue to follow the car's progress. Her gaze instinctively sought out Mae. And she saw the matriarch give one of her patented self-satisfied smiles.

"Oh, my golly!" Gib exclaimed as the car drew to a stop. "It's Gloria!"

CHAPTER TWELVE

TANNER STOOD UP, unable to believe what his eyes told him. Gloria was here?

He looked at Rafe, who seemed just as shocked as he was. But if neither of them had contacted her, then who…? Gloria wouldn't have come on her own.

Shannon pulled Nikki from the high chair and made her way to Rafe as speculation buzzed around the tables.

Tanner watched Gloria park what had to be a rental car and step out onto the drive.

His stepmother looked great in a powder blue suit that fitted her pleasing plumpness to perfection. And, as always, she might have just left the services of a fine beauty salon—her silvery hair teased high and sprayed, her makeup flawless.

Rafe had managed to gain his feet, ready to go intercept her, when Mae called to the new arrival, "You're just in time, Gloria. Barbecue's still hot. I thought for a bit you weren't goin' to make it."

The declaration silenced everyone.

Gloria smiled her wonderful smile, just as she'd done the first time Tanner had seen her when he and his brother and sisters had been told she was going to be their father's new wife. A couple of his older sisters had had a temporary problem with that, but Tanner never had. He'd wanted his dad to be happy, even at the young age of nine. He'd also wanted them to be a family again. And with Gloria's wonderful smile and warm personality, she'd made them just that.

"I'd almost forgotten how far this place is from everything!" she called back, laughter bubbling in her voice. She took in the astonishment on everyone's faces and said, "It's just little ol' me!"

She moved toward them with arms outstretched and hugged her way along the ends of the tables to where Mae sat.

Tanner went directly to greet her, and she gave him a special embrace, along with a quick examination that confirmed to him the depth of her concern about his well-being.

She greeted Rafe with another special embrace, moving on to Shannon and her three grandchildren.

"Oh, they've grown so!" she complained good-naturedly. "You're going to have to make them stop. Either that or get yourselves to Arizona more often."

Finally she turned to Mae and her high spirits faded.

Tanner saw Claire closing in from the outside. She moved, seemingly without effort, to a place where, if Mae needed her, she would be there.

Like two venerable combatants, Mae and Gloria looked each other up and down.

Mae commented first. "Well, you look just as nice as you always have."

"And you look—" Gloria began what must have been a false compliment, then spoke with complete honesty. "You don't look so good, Mae. You look tired."

Mae smiled—a brief pull of her lips—in appreciation of Gloria's candor. "I am tired most days. But not today. The fixin's are all in the usual place. Nothin's changed about that. We'll have our talk later. You are stayin' the night like I asked you to, aren't you?"

Gloria broke into a winsome smile. "You bet I am! The thought of getting back into that car is enough to give me the heebie-jeebies. And I'm starving! The only thing I've had since breakfast is one of those peanut packs they give you on the airplane."

Mae turned to Rafe. "Rafe, help your mother with—" Then she stopped. She didn't complete the directive.

Rafe was already taking his mother's arm and leading her to the serving table, while Harriet scooted his two boys down toward her so their grandmother would have a seat when she returned.

While Gloria greeted Axel like a long-lost relation, everyone else returned to their places and their meals.

"What's goin' on?" Jack asked, his voice muted, as Shannon slipped Nikki back into the high chair and sat down herself.

Shannon shrugged. She turned to Tanner. "Tanner, did you know about this?"

"Not a thing," he said.

Shannon knit her brow. "I wonder what Mae's up to."

"Whatever it is, she's sure the one callin' the shots," Jack proclaimed with a short laugh.

"And that's different?" Emma asked dryly.

Claire also reclaimed her place, but she made sure no portion of her body touched Tanner's.

Sporadic conversations carried on while everyone applied themselves to their dinner. All except for Claire. She did little more than pick at her meal.

"You don't like the barbecue?" Tanner asked quietly when those around them were either distracted or off for a second helping.

Her gaze remained on her plate. "No, it's very good. I'm just not—"

Tanner forked her almost untouched slice of beef and part of her mound of potato salad onto his plate.

He grinned. ''There. Now no one will know.''

The color in her cheeks heightened, but her only response was a brief nod. Finally she asked, ''Do we take our plates somewhere when we're finished?''

''Axel and Marie collect them when they bring dessert.''

Her eyes jerked up. ''Dessert!'' she echoed.

How had he thought to describe her as ''interesting'' or ''cute'' before? She was beautiful. He'd heard the cliché ''drowning in a woman's eyes,'' but he'd never expected to experience it. Her gray eyes were like pools, and he'd gladly fall into them and surrender...

He pulled himself back from the brink of doing something stupid by reminding himself of myriad complications in his life. Especially the latest, his stepmother's surprise visit.

''It's usually some of Axel's famous peach cobbler,'' he said, drawing his thoughts back to the subject of dessert. ''I couldn't get enough of it when I was a kid.''

''How long will that take?'' she asked.

Tanner smiled. She sounded as if anything past

five seconds would be too long. "They'll bring it when everyone's done."

Her gaze moved to Mae. Tanner had noticed her checking on the family matriarch more often since Gloria's arrival. Her face exhibited a growing concern.

"What is it?" he asked.

"I think Mae should rest."

"She seems to be having a good time."

"She is."

"Then what's the problem?"

Her gray eyes swung around to him, but she said nothing.

"Were you in on her plans for today?" he asked.

"Your stepmother? No."

"But you know something the rest of us don't. Does it have anything to do with why Gloria's here?"

Once again she merely looked at him.

Tanner returned the look. The voices and laughter surrounding them faded to a distant murmur. He lost track of everything but her. Seconds, minutes, hours could have passed—

An arm curved around his shoulders and Gloria's flowery perfume enveloped him.

"Well, are you going to introduce me?" she demanded from behind him. "Or do I have to introduce myself?"

By the time Tanner shook himself free, his stepmother had already taken the initiative.

"I'm Gloria Reid," she said, reaching past him with an extended right hand. "Rafe's mother and Tanner's stepmother. And you're Claire Hannaford. Mae told me about you while we were eating. She said to get Tanner to do the honors, but he seems...well, preoccupied."

Claire accepted Gloria's hand, her cheeks flushing a brighter pink.

Tanner saw the speculative spark that leaped into his stepmother's eyes. To prevent her from saying anything ill-timed—Gloria was an enthusiastic romantic—he said, "Mom, have you seen who's here? Jack Denton and Jim Cleary." He motioned to the men on the other side of the table.

Gloria gave a little yelp and abandoned what she'd been about to say. She hurried around the table to greet her old friends. "Ah, Jack! I haven't seen you in— You weren't able to get to Rafe and Shannon's wedding, were you? You were out on a call." She chortled joyfully. "You're looking good! Older, but good. And aren't we all getting older?" She turned from one hug to another. "And Jim! My goodness, Jim. I *did* see you at the wedding. But not since—"

She slipped into introspection, but quickly regained her smile as she moved down that side of the table to greet Emma Connelly, and finally Erin Hughes and Gwen Dunn.

The last time she'd seen the teenage girls, she exclaimed, was also at the wedding. Only then, Erin had been eight or nine years old and, with her mother, a new arrival at the ranch, and Gwen had barely been five.

Gloria's happiness warmed Tanner's heart. He'd known all along that she'd deeply missed her family and friends in West Texas. Yet she'd had no way to heal the rift except by admitting to Mae that she'd been wrong. And Gloria couldn't do that. Did Mae's invitation mean that the matriarch was finally ready to take the first step?

Tanner glanced at Claire again and was surprised to see that as pleased and hopeful as he felt, she felt just the opposite. She, too, had been watching his stepmother, but Gloria's happiness seemed to bring her distress.

He frowned, wanting to question her, but before he found a way, she vaulted to her feet and stepped over the bench.

"Claire?" he called after her as she started away from the table.

"I...have to go inside for a minute. If Mae needs me—"

"I'll come find you," he said.

She looked at him for the space of a heartbeat, then continued on her way. Tanner stared after her in confusion.

Why was she upset?

WHAT A PERSON doesn't have, they don't miss. What a person doesn't have—

Claire leaned her forehead against the closed parlor door and repeated the words under her breath.

Only the mantra no longer worked. She *did* miss what she didn't have. She missed having a family. She'd missed it all her life.

Mrs. Stanton had taught her the axiom when she'd been placed back in her care for a short period during her first year in school. The wonderful, caring woman must have seen how lonely she'd felt standing off to one side, watching while her school friends had been gathered into the protective arms of their families at the end of the day, and she had done her best to inoculate her against the pain. Claire hadn't made sense of the adage at first, but it had made her feel better. And slowly, over the years, she'd come to believe it.

A tear slipped down her cheek.

She'd believed it to the point where she'd convinced herself that her way was the better way. Especially after the debacle with the Fitzgeralds.

Maybe she *was* jealous of the Parkers. Not so much of their heritage, but of what they had now!

A second tear followed the first.

Gloria Reid had returned to the ranch after a long separation, assured that the majority of those living there would love and accept her…be happy to see her. And she'd been proved correct.

The Parkers came together with warmth and regard and enough love that it spilled over to estranged in-laws.

And where was she while all this happened? Off to one side, watching. Just as she had been all her life.

But that was where she *needed* to be, she told herself. She didn't have a family, and wanting one only brought dejection.

Claire sniffed and rubbed the moisture from her cheeks. Then she straightened her shoulders, ordered her expression and opened the hall door. Her duty was to the woman who'd brought her to this place. And Mae needed her outside.

MAE FINALLY CONSENTED TO rest as pallets were spread on the grass under a tree for the younger children. But she agreed only after strong assurances that no one would leave before her return.

''I know they're gonna talk about me,'' the matriarch grumbled to Claire as she accompanied her to the main house. "And I wanna know what they're sayin'. I feel just like a little kid again, havin' to take a nap in the middle of the afternoon."

"You must be worn out," Claire said diplomatically.

"Yeah, I guess I am," Mae admitted.

"Then rest, and you'll have more energy later."

Mae shot her a speculative glance. "I noticed that you disappeared earlier."

Claire steadied her charge over the surface change from courtyard grass to the driveway's hard-packed gravel. "There are private moments," she said quietly.

"Was that a 'private moment' I saw on your bodice when you came back? Looked like tear-stains to me."

"It's a warm day," Claire evaded, trying not to let Mae's perceptiveness disconcert her. "It feels good to splash water on your face."

"Some of it stayed in your eyes, too!"

"Mae—"

"All right, all right. Have it your way. But I know what I saw. And just in case you're wonderin', it wasn't enough for anyone else to notice. I just kinda put things together." She tilted her head. "What were you cryin' about, anyway? Did

Tanner say somethin' you took exception to? You two were talkin' all friendly like before you left.''

"I didn't say I cried."

Mae's pace slowed as they mounted the two porch steps, then slowed even more as they crossed to the front door. She stopped to take several short breaths.

Claire watched her in concern. The woman would never show weakness in front of her family, unless it was beyond her control. Claire castigated herself for not insisting that she go for a rest earlier.

Mae covered her inability to continue with a jaunty wave to family members who'd followed their progress to the house. Then the two women went inside. As soon as the door closed, Mae sagged against Claire, fully depleted.

"Marie!" Claire lifted her voice, careful not to be heard outside. "Marie…please. Are you there?"

Claire knew she could get the elderly woman to the bedroom unassisted, but it would be so much easier for Mae if Marie could help. Mae had no strength left to draw on.

The housekeeper hurried into the entryway, wiping her hands on her apron. She blanched when she saw what had happened, then went immediately to bolster Mae's other side. Together, the two women supported the matriarch to the bedroom and helped her stretch out on the bed.

"Just like a baby," Mae muttered, her eyelids fluttering shut.

"She's not—" Marie whispered with trepidation, her face starting to crumple.

"No. She's sleeping," Claire assured her softly, detecting the steady rise and fall of Mae's chest.

"Wore herself to a frazzle," Marie said sadly and shook her head. She watched as Claire covered the woman with a light blanket. "She was sure havin' a good time. Never have seen her have such a good one. Axel and me were talkin' about that earlier."

They moved quietly into the parlor.

"Thank you for coming so quickly, Marie."

"Glad to be of help. Would you like a nice glass of iced tea all to yourself? I'll be glad to getcha one."

Claire shook her head. "No...but thanks."

"Anytime you want somethin'," the woman stated firmly, "you just let me or Axel know. We'll be glad to get it, whatever it is."

As the housekeeper closed the door behind her, Claire knew Marie had just awarded her with her seal of approval.

LESS THAN A HALF HOUR later someone tapped on the door. Claire reluctantly set her notebook aside and went to answer it. She was surprised to find Gloria.

"I hope I'm not interrupting," the woman whispered as she peeked into the bedroom at Mae's sleeping form. "I was wondering...do you think we could talk for a few minutes? I have some questions, and Tanner told me I should ask you." She smiled hopefully.

Claire slipped into the hall, careful to keep the door partially ajar so she could hear Mae, if needed.

Gloria kept her voice hushed. "I'm not sure if you're aware of this or not, but Mae called a few days ago and asked me to visit. I tried to find out what was going on, but she wouldn't tell me. She just said to get myself here. That it was important. I booked a flight for Monday, the first day I could manage, then she called again yesterday afternoon and said I needed to be here today. Tomorrow wouldn't do." She paused for a breath. "Quite a change, I can tell you. Those were the first calls she's made to me in twenty-six years. I almost dropped the phone both times! She still wouldn't tell me what it was about, but from the way she acted, and when I got here— But never mind that. I'd better get to my questions." Her round face sobered. "What's wrong with her? I asked the family, but they don't seem to know much more than me. I know she's almost ninety-two, but they said she's passed out a couple of times. Is it her heart? I have a friend whose mother kept passing out and what she needed was a pacemaker. Her heart beat too slowly. Could that be what Mae—?''

''She's under a doctor's care,'' Claire cut in. ''If she needed a pacemaker, she'd have one.''

''But *would* she? Mae's a stubborn woman. She might refuse.''

Gloria's determined insistence gave Claire an inkling as to where Rafe had picked up his strong will even beyond his Parker genes.

Claire took a breath. ''She's just...wearing down. Of old age.''

For a moment Gloria was silent, then she asked, ''How should I go about doing this, then? Talking with her, I mean. She's told me she wants to meet with me as soon as the barbecue's over. What if she gets excited? Gets angry? Would that be bad for her? Harm her? Especially after such an exhausting day.'' She clasped Claire's forearm. ''Will you be there? I don't mind. I'm not ashamed of what I did. I fell in love with Patrick Reid when falling in love was the farthest thing from my mind. I went on a cruise to lift my spirits, Patrick and I met and—the rest, as they say, is history. I won't apologize for it. I loved Rafe's father. Loved him so much that when I lost him I didn't think I could ever love anybody again. But when I first saw Patrick on that ship— Tanner reminds me so much of him at that time. Same eyes, same smile, same—''

''It would be best not to upset her,'' Claire broke in hastily. ''Especially, as you say, after such a hectic day.''

''But what if I can't control it? Mae has her own ideas about things. She always has had. Will you be there?'' she repeated.

''That's up to Mae. But if not, I can be nearby if it makes you feel better.''

Gloria worried her bottom lip. ''We'll probably be in her office. That's where she always calls people on the carpet. Tries to intimidate them…and does a pretty good job of it.''

''But not with you.'' The words slipped out before Claire could stop them, and she immediately wished she had.

''So you know some of the ins and outs of what's happened,'' Gloria said, her green eyes narrowing. ''And you've only been here a week?''

''A lot has happened in this week.''

''So I gather. Tanner's been here a week, too.''

He arrived the day before me, Claire almost said, but didn't. She'd already piqued the woman's curiosity.

"He's been through a lot himself recently," Gloria said.

Claire remained silent.

"I've been worried about him. It was my idea that he come to the ranch to help Rafe. To get his mind off—"

When Gloria paused, Claire glanced back into the parlor, a signal that their conversation should end.

"Just how well do you know Tanner?" Gloria asked. When Claire's body instinctively tightened, the woman smiled. "Remember, I know what it's like to be bowled over by one of the Reid men."

Pushing the door open with the flat of her hand, Claire backed into the parlor. "I'll be outside the office later," she said.

The reference to the upcoming meeting set Gloria back on course. Her good-natured matchmaking abruptly halted.

"I sure miss coming to see my grandbabies," she said. "I hope that Mae— Well, I hope she's finally going to admit that I did the only thing I could at the time. Patrick and his kids needed me. And I needed them." She reached out to squeeze Claire's hand in thanks. "I'll tell the others what you said."

Claire nodded and closed herself back into the relative safety of the parlor.

CHAPTER THIRTEEN

MAE AWAKENED AFTER AN HOUR.

She still looked pale, and Claire tried to convince her to stay in bed longer, but Mae refused.

"Too much time's already been wasted," she declared, and after smoothing her hair back into its topknot and patting some color into her cheeks, she proclaimed herself ready to go.

As promised, none of the family or friends had left the gathering. The toddlers continued to sleep on their shaded pallets, the older children played in one of the houses, and the adults had pulled the chairs into a wide circle so they could talk in a single group.

Wes vacated a chair for Mae, then sprawled on the grass. Tanner did the same for Claire.

"We were just rememberin' that play wedding Gwen and Wes and Erin set up the month before Rafe and Shannon were married," Harriet said, catching them up on the conversation. She turned to Delores Hughes. "Jessica was involved in that, too, wasn't she?"

The woman smiled. "She made sure *she* was the bride."

"What's Jessica up to now?" LeRoy asked.

"Makin' sure she's still the bride. We got a letter from Russell today. Jessica and her boyfriend ran off last weekend and got married in Las Vegas. Didn't tell anybody anything, most especially her daddy. It also seems we're goin' to be great-grandparents!"

Offers of congratulations were delivered from all around.

"Erin was the minister that day," Harriet said, carrying on with her memories. "Gwen the flower-girl, and Wes the groom. The groom who disrupted everything, then ran off, with the girls chasin' after him. You were so mad at him, remember?" she prompted "the girls."

"I wanted to do him in," Gwen muttered, and playfully tapped a foot against her older brother's back.

"I mostly remember us havin' to clean up after," Wes drawled. "All those dolls and stuffed animals sittin' in chairs in the backyard, with flowers and stuff scattered around. Whose idea was all that, anyway?"

"At least you didn't have to do that *and* wash a bunch of makeup off your face," Gwen retorted. "Some of it wouldn't come off!"

"I'll go find the photos," Harriet volunteered, standing up. "You never saw 'em, did you, Gloria? They're great. The kids were so cute!"

Wes groaned at his mother's effusiveness.

"See?" LeRoy nudged his son's boot with his own. "I knew those pictures would come back to getcha one day."

"I think they're sweet," Erin said softly.

"I do, too," Mae agreed, and patted her hand.

The yellow Labrador trotted up as the children changed houses, moving from Harriet and LeRoy's place to play at Rafe and Shannon's.

The dog thrust his nose at several people to say hello, and when he found Rafe, he wagged his tail even harder. Then he moved over to where Tanner had stretched out on the grass. Again, he wagged his tail in greeting and, because Tanner was within easy reach, added several quick licks to his face.

"Junior!" Rafe corrected him.

The dog's head jerked up.

Tanner laughed as he wiped his cheek. "What's a little face washing between friends, huh, boy?" He rubbed the Labrador's ears, and the dog curled on the grass beside him.

Claire couldn't pull her eyes away from the pair...until Tanner looked up.

Marie brought bowls and spoons to the serving table. "Axel's got a surprise," she announced.

"He's made ice cream! We thought since we haven't done it yet this summer, for one reason or another, y'all might like a little taste." The announcement was met with wholehearted enthusiasm.

Axel followed a distance behind his wife, carrying a big old-fashioned hand-crank ice cream maker in a galvanized tub. He placed the tub on the ground not far from the group.

"It's been settin' up for a while, so it should be just right for eatin'," he said, grinning.

"I'll get some for you, Aunt Mae," Erin volunteered, ready to jump up from her chair next to the matriarch.

Mae held her back. "You're a good girl, Erin. I'm proud you're one of us. You know that, don't you?"

"And I'm proud of you," Erin said softly.

Mae smiled and let her go.

As if by some kind of internal detector, the children burst out of Rafe and Shannon's house, yelling, "Ice cream! Ice cream!"

Harriet returned with the photos at the same time.

Everyone seemed happy and relaxed as they chatted, ate ice cream and looked at Harriet's photos. Only the toddlers, awakened by the commotion, were out of sorts. But spoonfuls of the surprise dessert soon took care of that.

Mae didn't seem to notice, as Claire did, the effort put forth by the various family members. From the slight strain at the edges of their relaxed good humor, she concluded that Gloria had passed along the information, and that they all must have decided to keep their knowledge from Mae.

The effort seemed most difficult for Jodie. But she wouldn't allow her fears to cast a pall on this day when Mae's happiness was so apparent.

Claire stayed in close range of her charge as the afternoon wore on, alert for signs of increasing weakness.

But Mae was amazing. She never flagged. Without really seeming to make a point of it, she had a special word with each individual, including the children.

Then, finally, the group broke up. Those who lived off the ranch compound were waved away in their various vehicles by those who didn't. Everyone seemed loath to see the afternoon end. Remaining family members pitched in to help the Douglases clear the courtyard.

Once that activity began, Mae turned to Gloria and said, "Well, we can't put this off any longer, can we? Come to my office and we'll have our talk."

Gloria's eyes sought out Claire, and within seconds the three women made their way inside the main house.

Claire hung back outside the office door, and when Mae gave no sign of calling her in, she took it that the matriarch wanted to be alone with her estranged niece-by-marriage. Mindful of her promise, though, Claire remained in the hall.

Various Parkers passed in and out through the front door, returning glasses, dishes and chairs that had been used outdoors.

Once, Claire heard Tanner's voice.

She'd tried very hard *not* to be aware of him all afternoon, but she'd known where he was every second.

The office door swung open far sooner than Claire expected, and Gloria stepped out. She seemed stunned by what had occurred. But a broad smile soon brightened her round face.

"Mae apologized," she said in amazement. "*Mae* apologized. She told me she'd been wrong all these years. I can't believe it!"

She hugged Claire impulsively and hurried down the hall, still expressing her disbelief.

Stepping over to the open office door, Claire peered inside. Mae stood at her desk—her white head bowed, her hands outspread on its surface.

She looked beyond exhaustion, as if the desk was the only thing that kept her upright.

"You shouldn't push yourself so hard," Claire chided gently as she hurried inside. "What would it hurt if you'd put this meeting off until tomorrow? Gloria's staying the night."

The matriarch was silent as Claire helped her into the next room.

"It was such a nice day," Mae breathed as she collapsed onto the bed.

Once Claire had slipped off Mae's shoes, she quickly set about easing away her outer clothing. Then she ran warm water into a bowl and gave her a simple sponge bath.

"Mmm, that feels good," Mae murmured. "Felt good to mend things with Gloria, too. I never shoulda did what I did to her."

Claire slipped a cotton nightgown she'd found in a bottom drawer over Mae's head and helped her under the cover. Then she released her hair from its upswept knot, letting it fall over the pillow.

"You should sleep now," she advised gently, awed by this woman's sheer determination.

"There's some letters over there—" Mae tried to sit up, pointing to her vanity table.

Claire settled her back down. "That's enough for one day," she said.

Mae's fingers caught at her arm. "I want— If somethin' happens…I want you to give 'em to Rafe. Promise me you'll give 'em to Rafe!"

"I promise," Claire said over a tight throat.

And moments later, as she left the room, she had to wipe away a tear.

"I CAN'T BELIEVE IT," Gloria said in continued amazement as she sank onto the straight-backed chair Tanner had just brought into the house. "It's over. I'm back in the fold. She told me that Patrick and I should come visit anytime we want." She looked at Shannon, on her way to the kitchen with an armload of soiled tablecloths. "You and Rafe and the kids won't be the only ones traveling now."

"I'm happy for you, Mom," Tanner said, and bent to kiss her cheek.

"But will Patrick come?" Shannon asked seriously.

Patrick Reid had taken up his wife's cause, and for years been angry with Mae for the distress her long-term grudge had caused Gloria.

"Oh, he'll come," Gloria said firmly.

"Or wish he had!" Rafe laughed as he brought in another chair.

Tanner started back outside, but Rafe stopped him.

"That's the last for this house," he said. "And the rest'll all be done by the time you get out there."

Shannon returned from the kitchen and slipped easily into place by Rafe's side. "That's it for me, too," she said. "Marie's been washing dishes all along and won't hear of help with the last part." She glanced at Tanner and Gloria. "After the kids get their baths, why don't you two come over and spend a little time with us? Gloria, you can see what we've done with the place since you and Ward used to live there."

"We'd *love* to," Gloria answered happily for both of them.

Rafe grinned and clapped Tanner on the back, then left the house with his wife.

"They look happy," Gloria said, her eyes following the pair into the entryway. "I am, too. I know it shouldn't matter so much. Sometimes when people dig in their heels and won't budge, you just have to leave them behind. But there was always this ache inside." She tapped her chest lightly. "I've always felt a part of the Parker Ranch. Ward...he was just like Rafe is now...it was in his blood. A little bit of it must've got in mine, too. More than I ever imagined. And Mae—darn her cantankerous hide!—I still love her. I did, even when I didn't want to."

"I know."

Gloria cocked her head. "You do?"

"I know you." Tanner smiled at his stepmother as he offered her a hand up. "Mae's put you in the same room you and Dad used when you came for the wedding."

Gloria grinned. "It had twin beds. Patrick was furious. He took it as a planned slight from Mae."

"I never knew that."

"It didn't work out so bad. We shared one of the beds and by the next morning he'd forgotten all about being angry."

"So that's why he was wearing that silly grin all day," Tanner teased. "I wondered."

Gloria playfully slapped his arm. "Now I *know* you're fibbing!"

When they stepped into the entryway on their way upstairs to freshen up, Tanner couldn't prevent a glance down the long hall toward Mae's bedroom. Claire had been on guard all afternoon—in the background, but near at hand. He felt positive she was with Mae now.

"She's a pretty little thing," Gloria said, noticing where his attention wandered.

"Mmm-hmm," Tanner agreed.

"Quiet. Professional."

They started up the stairs.

"She's very into doing her job," Tanner said.

"You've tried to take her away from it?" Gloria guessed. "Did you succeed?"

When he didn't answer, his stepmother declared, "She's crazy if she let's you get away."

"Mom...you're prejudiced."

"I am! But I also know a good man when I see one."

Tanner accompanied her to the door of her temporary quarters. "We'll give the kids about a half hour, don't you think?"

"That should be fine," Gloria agreed. "I don't want to be so late they're already asleep." Then she paused, as if realization once again hit. "But then...I can visit them as often as I want to now. Isn't that wonderful?"

MAE ALLOWED HERSELF TO BE served breakfast in bed the next morning, and at the finish, pronounced that she'd enjoyed the experience. Especially when Claire joined her with toast and coffee in the bedside chair.

Her stay in bed didn't last, though. She had plans for the new day, she said. Last night's vulnerability had been forgotten, or at least suppressed.

Mae and Claire joined the small group that saw Gloria off for the airport—waving at the maroon sedan until it could no longer be seen. Then Mae turned to Rafe and Tanner and fixed them with a steely gaze.

"Tanner, go find Gib and tell him I need to see him in my office at ten-thirty on the dot. Rafe, you be there at eleven."

Rafe protested. "Aunt Mae, I have to get that water tank cleaned sometime."

"Another few hours won't hurt anything. I won't keep you long."

She then tucked her free arm through Claire's and together they returned to her office. Claire assumed she would be given an assignment as well, but was surprised when Mae fluttered her fingers and told her she had a call to make.

A short time later she called Claire back into the room. From her scowl, Claire could see that the call had not gone as expected.

At exactly ten-thirty Gib tapped on the door. Claire stood up, waiting to be dismissed again, but Mae did no such thing.

Claire smiled faintly at Gib and backed away so he could have a measure of privacy with his aunt.

Gib seemed to resent neither her presence nor the command appearance. If anything, he welcomed both.

"I'm sure you can guess what this is about,"

Mae began, her frown returning in full force. "It's that lady friend of yours."

"Lurleen." Gib supplied the name. "And she's my fiancée."

"She must hide her tracks pretty well. John Fellows can't find a thing on her."

"That's because there's nothin' to find," Gib answered mildly. "She doesn't have any tracks—not the kind you're talkin' about."

"So it seems," Mae muttered.

"She's a good woman, Aunt Mae. I'm not gonna find me another bad one. I've been through that. I know better."

Mae held on stubbornly. "She could be after your money...your share in the ranch."

"She's got all the money she wants. Her husband left her comfortable. John Fellows had to have told you that. As for the ranch...she'll sign any papers you want renouncin' my share if I go first."

"You've talked about this?" Mae asked.

"She's already been to her lawyer."

Mae was silent a moment, then demanded, "How'd you meet her?"

"I was wonderin' when you'd get around to askin' me that." Gib grinned. "I've known her for years. Met her at the art supply store up in Fort Stockton when I first started paintin'."

"Mighta known it would have somethin' to do with paintin'," Mae grumbled.

Gib waited as his aunt considered the matter. Finally, her frown cleared and she said, "All right. You know I was only tryin' to make sure you weren't gonna do somethin' stupid again. You're too good a man to have people take advantage of you, Gib. You should be happy. And if this woman makes you happy—"

Gib whooped his elation.

Mae actually smiled. She stood up and tapped around the desk until she stood beside her nephew. Then she hugged him awkwardly and patted his back. "One bit of advice, son, now that things are settled. Don't wait too long. No use wastin' time. There won't be any papers for Lurleen to sign."

"I never thought—" Gib began, beaming.

"That was the problem," Mae cut in dryly. Then she shooed him away. "Now go on back to whatever you were doin'."

"Thanks, Aunt Mae," Gib said gratefully.

The matriarch resettled at her desk and picked up a letter. As soon as Gib closed the door, she set it aside.

"What about a rest?" Claire urged, noting, as she drew closer, that Mae's lips were tinged with gray.

Mae rejected the idea. "Don't have time. Rafe's comin'."

"What you did just now," Claire said. "It was very nice."

The older woman made a sound deep in her throat, but all she said was, "If you want to do somethin' for me, bring me that photo album."

Claire did as she requested and sat on the couch—pencil and notepad at hand—while Mae slowly turned the pages of the thick book.

At exactly eleven o'clock Rafe rapped on the door and strode into the office without waiting for a signal to enter. His frown matched Mae's in intensity.

She looked him straight in the eye. "When are you goin' to show me those records you've been workin' on? I know what you and Tanner have been up to. And, no, he didn't tell me. I just know what *I'd* do."

"Twenty minutes okay?" Rafe shot back, seemingly not at all taken aback by her knowledge.

"How far along is he?" she demanded.

"As far as I told him to go."

"All of it?"

"No, just a part. I knew if I could get you to look at a sample, you'd be convinced."

Mae tipped her head. "Does it save a lot of time?"

"And trouble."

"You like it? You like what you've seen?"

"I liked it the first time I saw it at Jim's place."

Mae didn't miss a beat. "Then do what you think best."

Rafe said nothing, possibly in shock.

"What's the matter, boy?" Mae prodded. "You hard a' hearing?"

Rafe didn't seem to believe what he'd heard. He continued trying to convince her. "Tanner says all we have to do is somethin' called a *save,* and somethin' else called a *backup,* and we won't lose anythin'. He's teachin' me how to do it all. And Shannon says she'll help, too."

Mae nodded.

For the first time since Claire had met the impressive manager of the Parker Ranch, Rafe seemed a little uncertain.

"It's important to keep up with things," Mae said, breaking the silence. "Look at all the cattle diseases we have a handle on today. My daddy woulda give his right arm to be able to do what we can. If usin' a computer makes the ranch run better, use it. It's one thing to keep to tradition, and somethin' else entirely not to take advantage of progress. I forgot that for a little while. You didn't."

"New ways are hard to get used to sometimes," Rafe suggested gruffly.

Mae smiled slightly. "Yes, but sometimes it's because somebody has too hard a head. Remember that yourself, Rafe."

He smiled slightly. "Yes, ma'am."

"Now go clean that water tank." Mae waved him away.

Once he'd gone, Mae lost a lot of her steam. "I think I'm goin' to have me that rest now, Claire. All of a sudden I just—"

Claire helped her to the bedroom without comment.

"You're very sweet," Mae said, her dark eyes watching Claire as she once again tucked her into bed.

"You are, too," Claire said, and meant it.

"No, I'm not. Not for a day in my life. I always wished I could be, but— You play the hand you're given, don't you? And you do your best with it. It's always important to do your best."

The words trailed away as her eyelids grew heavy.

You play the hand you're given....

That's what Claire had done her entire life.

CLAIRE FINISHED READING the family history while Mae slept, and at the end she felt immersed in cattle drives, droughts, oil and natural gas wells, and improvements in animal and land husbandry. She could understand a little better the Parkers' deep abiding love for this place. To them, the ranch was a living entity that demanded, and received, their undying loyalty. They *were* the ranch, and the ranch was them.

She slid the book onto the end of her narrow bed, ready to return it when Mae awakened. She moved restlessly around the room, then to the door. She had to get out of here, if only for a few minutes.

The painting in the living room drew her. She'd noted it, but never really examined it.

As she'd been told, the subject was ranch headquarters, from the perspective of a low rising hill. All the houses in the compound were there, the work buildings, the pens and corrals.

Just a short time ago she'd never heard of the Parker Ranch. Now she was going to have a hard time dismissing it from her mind. Just as she would all the people here. And Tanner— She didn't want to think of Tanner!

"That's a real place, you know," Mae said from close behind her. "Gib caught it just right."

Claire spun around guiltily. "I didn't mean to be away when you woke up!"

"I can still do for myself."

She turned back to the painting. "It's from a beautiful vantage point."

"Yes. Has Tanner been in for lunch yet?"

"Uh, no, I— Not that I know of."

"Then you can find him on your way to bring the Cadillac around. He's probably in the ranch office. I want to show you that spot where this picture was painted, and I want to see it myself. Used to go there most every day. It's been too long since I've been." Melancholia crept into her voice.

"Tanner?" Claire echoed, taking in little beyond the fact that she'd been told to find him.

"I want him to come with us. We're gonna need his brawn."

With all the Parker men around, couldn't they find someone else? But Claire knew better than to argue. Mae wanted what she wanted, and she almost always got it.

CHAPTER FOURTEEN

"YOU CAN PUT ME DOWN HERE," the matriarch said from her secure position in Tanner's arms.

"I don't recall ever being up here before, Mae," he said as he set her easily on her feet.

"Probably weren't."

"I heard about cemetery hill, though."

Mae planted her cane on the hard ground and stepped through a gap in the low picket fence that encased a number of headstones.

Claire, the last to crest the hill, took a moment to scan the valley spread out before them. It was exactly like viewing Gib's painting of ranch headquarters—the houses, the work buildings, the pens and corrals. Only this was real.

"Come on," Mae called over her shoulder, encouraging them to follow her example.

Before doing her bidding, Tanner relieved Claire of the wicker basket she'd carried from the car. When their hands touched in the transfer, Claire quickly withdrew hers.

"You'll see some familiar names here," Mae said, once they'd joined her inside the fence. She gestured to the markers—some very old. "There's Virgil and Gibson, Deena and Sue, my daddy and mama, my brothers, Rafe's daddy."

The headstones were a roll call of the Parkers who'd worked so hard to carve this ranch out of miles of harsh, rugged land. Watt, Mae's father, rested forever next to his wife, Martha. Theodore, their older son, was nearby, with his rank and the battle in which he'd been killed during the waning days of World War I carved into the stone.

Claire bent to remove a stray tuft of grass from the base of Theodore's headstone, then removed another tuft from Gibson's.

These people were no longer names in a book to her, or faces in long-ago photographs. She felt as if, in some small way, she knew them.

When she looked up, she saw that Mae had been watching her. She quickly straightened.

"It's like a Who's Who of the Parkers," Tanner remarked as he moved from spot to spot.

"The early ones who stayed on the ranch are all here," Mae confirmed.

Claire came upon a marker that stated, Infant Daughter, and was dated May 1889. Another said, Infant Son, dated two years later. She wanted to ask whose children they were, but she didn't trust her voice.

The summer sun beat down on them and Mae suggested a retreat to the wrought-iron bench set under a natural grouping of trees that shared the hill with the cemetery.

Mae seemed to be tiring, but she wouldn't hear of Tanner carrying her across the short distance. She didn't object, though, when both he and Claire took an arm.

The bench wasn't long enough for three.

"You two ladies have the bench," Tanner said quickly. "I'll just hunker down over here."

Mae's lips twitched as she gratefully took a seat. "A computer whiz knowin' how to hunker down. We're gonna make a cowboy outta you yet, boy!"

Tanner grinned and set the basket between them.

Though Mae's request for a picnic lunch had been made on the spur of the moment, Marie had packed the basket with an abundance of food. Sandwiches, leftover fried chicken, salads, fruit and cookies, cans of cold drinks.

"I'm not really much of a computer whiz," Tanner said as he chose a piece of chicken and a Coke. "I know how to make one do what I want, but—" He shrugged.

"That's more than Rafe knows," Mae grumbled.

"Not anymore. He's learning."

"He was spoutin' off silly words to me this mornin'," Mae said, and took a bite of her sliced turkey sandwich.

"I heard about that," Tanner replied.

Mae arched an eyebrow at him. "I should be mad at you for doin' what you did."

"But you're not." Tanner flashed a smile that made Claire's heart quiver.

"No, I'm not," Mae agreed.

Claire felt Tanner's gaze move to her and stay. She'd been eating her sandwich very quietly, trying not to draw attention to herself. Earlier, on her way to find him in the ranch office to deliver Mae's request, she'd decided there was only one way to get through this—she had to become as invisible as possible.

"You approve of what I did with Gloria, too?" Mae demanded of him.

He nodded. "I do."

Mae grew quiet at that point, and they finished their meal in silence.

Claire packed the debris from their lunch into the basket and waited for Mae's next move. Tanner stood up and started to walk around.

For a long time Mae didn't stir. Then she finally said, "You two go off on a walk or somethin'. I want to be on my own here for a while."

Claire froze. *Why* did Mae keep doing this? Pushing them together.

"Go on," Mae said, and waggled her fingers at them.

"How long is 'a while'?" Tanner asked.

"Claire'll know," Mae said.

When Claire began to protest, Tanner took her arm and propelled her back along the stony incline they'd climbed from the car.

"I don't—" she began

"You heard what she said. She wants to be alone. This place is special to her."

"I know that."

"Then act as if you do."

Claire shook off his grip and stopped. "I was going to say—I don't know if it's wise for us to go very far."

He glanced up to the sky. "It's going to get hot just standing here. Is the car too far?"

Claire looked around. There was nowhere else shaded for them to wait. Only low brush and grass and cactus and rocks. "No," she answered in frustration.

"Mae's a smart lady. She'll stay where she is."

He took several steps toward the car, then stopped to glance back to where Claire had remained stock-still. He flashed that smile again. "I promise. You can have the whole back seat to yourself.''

''Promises don't mean a thing to me,'' she muttered, and this time started to follow him.

At the car he swept open the back door and bowed her inside with an exaggerated flourish. He took the front passenger seat, but turned so he could see her. The car was old enough not to have headrests, so his view was unobstructed. He said nothing, merely looked at her.

Highly uncomfortable, Claire demanded, ''Did you get your tetanus booster?''

''I did. Want to feel the knot on my arm?'' A moment passed, then he asked, ''What did you mean when you said promises don't mean a thing to you?''

''They just don't.''

''Why not?'' he asked easily. ''Someone promise you something when you were a kid and it didn't happen?'' When Claire didn't respond, he peered into the back seat and said dryly, ''I don't see anybody back there with you.''

Once again Claire remained silent.

''Tell me about when you were a kid,'' he persisted. ''Where'd you live? What did your parents do? I've told you about mine and you've met my stepmother.'' His lightheartedness dropped away. ''Has someone hurt you that badly, Claire? Bad enough to steal your smiles? He must've been a really stupid bastard.''

"You don't know what you're talking about," she said unevenly.

"I know enough to know I don't want you hurt.''

"We've only known each other a week!''

"A week and a day," he corrected. "My dad and Gloria had it figured out in less time than that."

Claire fumbled for the door handle.

"Do you always run from the things that upset you?" he called after her when she erupted from the car.

She stopped near the top of the hill. She didn't want Mae to see her in this state—her face flushed, her breathing hurried, her emotions a shamble.

He had no right to say what he had! Asking about her private life, ridiculing her feelings!

Tanner mounted the hill at a slower pace, but he wasn't far behind.

Claire waited. She wanted to get whatever it was they were dealing with over once and for all.

"I don't have a family," she stated tautly when he stopped next to her. "Not a mother, not a father, a brother, a sister. Not a grandmother or an aunt. I'm on my own. I have been all my life."

For once he didn't have a snappy comeback.

She enjoyed her victory for a moment, then grew horrified at what she'd revealed.

"What I said earlier—" he began at last.

"Is perfectly all right! *I'm* perfectly all right. I don't need anything from anyone. Particularly promises!"

He held her gaze. "I keep my promises, Claire."

She whirled around, took a breath, reordered her expression and topped the rise.

"Are you ready to go home?" she asked Mae once she arrived at the bench.

If she'd noticed that Mae sat with her eyes partially closed, Claire wouldn't have snatched the woman so abruptly from her private world.

Mae looked at her blankly, but in the end nodded.

To make amends, Claire smiled as she helped the woman to her feet and handed her the black cane.

Tanner arrived seconds later, his features tight. With little effort he lifted the elderly woman into his arms and started down the hill.

MAE STAYED IN HER ROOM for most of the afternoon. Sometimes sleeping, sometimes leafing through the pages of the photo album.

Later, she sat on the front porch, watching the children play and listening to their chatter. Shannon and Harriet dropped by; Jodie called on the phone, as did Christine. "A nice afternoon," Mae deemed it.

For Claire, that time had been a torture. Especially when Tanner and Rafe returned from the work area and made themselves at home on the porch. She endured Tanner's long looks, and wished she could take back everything she'd said.

At last Mae grew weary and the two of them went inside.

"I think I'm goin' to have me another early night," the woman said as Claire closed the bedroom door. Yet she seemed reluctant to get into bed.

Claire helped her into her favorite tailored pajamas. "Would you like some warm milk? Some tea? Or—"

"Would you brush my hair?" Mae requested. "My mama used to do that, and I remember how nice it felt."

"Of course," Claire agreed. "In bed? Or at the vanity?"

Mae indicated the vanity.

Claire let down Mae's hair, then pulled the soft-bristled brush through the long white wisps. Lifting it, smoothing it and, she hoped, soothing away whatever concerned her.

"I had a gentleman friend once, you know,"

Mae surprised her by saying. "Almost married him. Had my bag packed and was on the verge of leavin' the ranch."

"You were leaving the ranch?" Claire echoed, even more surprised.

"Yes. But that's what stopped me. He couldn't live here, and I figured out I couldn't live in Houston. So I didn't do it."

"Does it make you sad sometimes to think about it?"

"Used to. Once in a while."

Claire continued the long gentle strokes.

"That's so nice," Mae murmured appreciatively.

"Mmm," Claire agreed. She could feel some of the tension ease from her charge's shoulders.

"I have somethin' for you," Mae said once she'd told her to stop. "It's on the bedside table."

Claire saw only the usual items.

"The book," Mae explained.

"That's the family history."

"I know. I want you to have it."

"But—"

"Claire," Mae said, turning to look at her intently. "I want you to have it. I wrote somethin' inside. Just for you."

"Mae, I— Thank you. Thank you," she repeated.

She spoke over the lump in her throat and around a heart that finally gave up its fight against the warm regard she'd come to feel for this special woman. She knew what the family history meant to Mae. Knew what it meant that she'd been given one of the few remaining copies.

Claire longed to show her gratitude with more than words. As if sensing this, Mae opened her arms.

Tears blurred Claire's vision as the once strong arms gathered her close.

Sniffing, she pulled away. "I'm sorry. I don't imagine you expected—"

"I didn't expect anything less." Mae's dark eyes had warmed. "You need a family, Claire. A family of your own. Don't close yourself off so much that you don't see what's in front of you. I've noticed the way you and Tanner look at each other. If I just had some more time— I don't regret what I did when I stayed put on the ranch. I took care of it and my family. Bein' here was what I was supposed to do. But you— If you don't have a family, girl, *make* yourself one!"

Mae hugged her again, patted her damp cheek, then said, "Now, I'm kinda tired, honey. I need to get some rest. We'll talk about this more in the mornin', all right?"

Claire turned down the bedcover and helped

Mae under the sheets. Then, after retrieving the family history from the bedside table and hugging it to her breast, she offered the older woman a tremulous smile and left the room.

THE NEXT MORNING CLAIRE awoke to an unusual brightness. Her first reaction was to check the clock, and she discovered it was a full hour later than Mae usually slept. The matriarch had said she was tired.

Claire donned her slippers and robe and moved quietly into the doorway that separated the two rooms.

Mae's supine form lay under the bedcover.

Claire watched for a moment, wondering whether to wake her charge. Then her body tautened.

She knew death. Knew its stillness.

Her stomach sank. Her heart twisted.

"No!" she whispered.

She moved to the bed on hollow legs.

Mae never stirred, her aged face peaceful.

Claire touched the side of her neck, felt the coolness, detected no pulse. She drew a ragged breath and checked again. Tears gathered in her eyes.

Someone tapped on the hall door and cracked it open. Marie!

The housekeeper started to say something, also

questioning the unusual lateness of the hour, when she saw Claire's expression and knew right away what had happened.

"Aw, no. No. No!" she breathed, and her knees buckled.

Claire hurried to her side, able to catch her before she collapsed to the floor.

The woman continued to moan.

Claire looked around. She needed to tell someone in the family. But no one was there to care for Marie.

Her own heart ached as she shut the hall door behind them and helped the woman into the living room and onto a sofa. Rafe was the person she needed to talk to. Only she couldn't telephone him with the news. She had to tell him in person.

"Marie...I have to find Rafe. Will you be all right if I leave you here?"

The housekeeper waved her away with the hand not clutching a handkerchief to her face. "Yes, tell Rafe," she agreed. "He'll know what to do."

It was after nine o'clock. Claire knew Rafe wouldn't be at his home.

"Where is he, do you know?" she asked the grieving woman.

"Tanner...Tanner said they'd be at the ranch office this mornin' when I—when I saw him earlier."

Claire changed quickly into her uniform, then hurried out the front door and down the path.

She knew she had to hold on to her emotions. She couldn't let herself react. Notifying the next of kin was as much a part of her job as caring for a failing patient. Normally, she did it with compassion and care...but at a distance. Now there was no distance at all. And it hurt!

Claire saw the two men in the ranch office. Rafe sat in front of the computer, Tanner stood at his side. She took a deep breath, composed her face and stepped onto the porch.

Both men looked up when she entered the room—Tanner with a leftover smile from something Rafe had said, and Rafe with immediate understanding.

"Is it Aunt Mae?" he asked huskily.

Claire nodded. "I'm very sorry. When I went to her room this morning—" Her throat tightened despite her self-discipline. "She passed away sometime in the night. In her sleep. Very peacefully."

Rafe looked stricken, but he didn't break down. Tanner braced his stepbrother's shoulders.

"I have to call Tate," Rafe said, and reached for the phone.

Claire knew the process. Notify local law enforcement, who brought in a member of the judiciary for the legal pronouncement...

Tanner came to her side. "Are you all right?" he asked in concern. "You look—"

"I have to be all right," she said tightly.

He put his hand on her shoulder. She left it there for a second before shrugging it away.

Rafe stood away from the desk once he hung up. "Who else knows?" he asked Claire.

"Marie."

"Well, you go back to her, and I'll tell everyone else." He dragged a hand through his hair. "This sure isn't going to be easy."

"What can I do to help?" Tanner asked.

Mae's death had rattled Rafe. He visibly had to pull himself together. "Go tell the hands that are close by. But give me about fifteen minutes. I want the others to know first." Then he stuffed his hat on his head and strode out of the office.

Claire glanced at Tanner, and without saying anything else, she abandoned the office herself.

CHAPTER FIFTEEN

A PALL FELL OVER THE entire ranch as word spread about Mae's death. Tate and Jodie arrived—little Megan stayed with Tate's mother. The Hugheses arrived, as did Jim Cleary. Family and close friends came together, mourned together. Even the younger children were subdued.

Claire did her best to help Marie and Axel. The pair insisted upon putting aside their grief in order to be of service to the surviving Parkers. Food appeared. Numerous pots of coffee, glasses of iced tea and lemonade.

As word spread farther afield, the telephones in the compound rang off their hooks with offers of condolence. A message even arrived from the governor's mansion in Austin.

In the middle of the afternoon Claire tapped on Mae's office door. Rafe's gruff voice bade her enter.

He sat at his great-aunt's desk but didn't look comfortable there. The weight of responsibility had borne down hard on him. He appeared exhausted.

"What can I do for you?" he asked.

Claire crossed the room to extend a small stack of letters. "Mae asked me to give these to you," she said quietly.

Rafe frowned as he accepted them. "When did she do this?"

"Night before last. She told me they were in one of her vanity drawers."

He sifted through the envelopes, looking at the names written in his great-aunt's hand. When he came to the one addressed to him, he let it slip free onto the desk's polished surface. "She tell you what's in them?" he asked.

"No, but I imagine—"

"I can, too."

He freed the flap and unfolded the sheet of quality notepaper. It didn't seem to matter that Claire was still there. Either Rafe was beyond caring that he'd once considered her an interloper, or he, like the others, had finally become completely accustomed to her presence.

Claire remained very still as he read the note.

Finally, he looked up and said flatly, "She wants Shannon and me to move into this house. I don't know if Shannon will do it."

"Mae once told me that you'd outgrown your place."

His dark eyes—so much like Mae's eyes—narrowed.

"That's why Tanner stayed here...in the main house," she said.

Rafe had always been an unknown quantity to her, and now he was fully in charge of everything.

"I—I also came to tell you that if Axel would put my trunk on top of my car, I can leave in the next hour. I just have to put away a few things."

"Are you in a hurry to leave?" he asked bluntly.

"I— No—"

"I'd've thought you'd want to hang around long enough to say goodbye to her."

Claire stared back at him. "You mean, stay for her service?"

He nodded.

"Well, yes, I'd like that. But—"

"Then stay. Mae liked you. Everyone likes you. You seem to have a calming influence, which is somethin' we could use quite a bit of right now."

"I didn't think you—" She stopped herself, concerned that he might not understand.

He waited for her to finish.

"I didn't think *you* liked me."

He smiled slightly. "Mae and I locked horns about plenty of things. She was one *stubborn* woman. But the best move she made lately was to hire you. She knew what she was doin'. Like she usually did.''

He stood up and held out a hand.

Claire rocked back on her heels. She never expected—never even *thought*—that Rafe Parker would take the time, particularly now, to thank her.

She returned his firm handshake.

And the phone rang. Again.

His lips tightened as he looked down at it. ''Probably the funeral home director,'' he said flatly. ''Donald said he'd call right back.''

Which cleared up a question in Claire's mind— why Rafe had closeted himself away from his family for the past hour. He'd wanted to be alone so he could make Mae's final arrangements.

CLAIRE DID ALL SHE COULD to help the family for the remainder of the day, mindful of what Rafe had said about her ''calming influence.'' More neighbors and associates from outside the ranch called or stopped by throughout the afternoon.

Finally, the long day ended and, after nightfall, the family members returned to their various houses.

Claire was exhausted as well as she made her way upstairs. Axel had moved her wardrobe trunk to the second bedroom, her new temporary quarters.

She didn't unpack any of her keepsakes, but she did examine the one item she'd be taking with her from the ranch—her copy of the Parker family history.

Last night she hadn't read the inscription Mae had written, but she wanted to do so now. She opened the book.

Nothing is impossible to a willing heart.
Claire, *you* have a willing heart.

She could almost hear Mae saying the words.

Sinking onto the end of the nearest bed, Claire again hugged the book to her breast, her eyes swimming.

Mae had also said, "If you don't have a family, girl, make yourself one!"

Only Mae didn't know that she'd already tried. And failed miserably. She'd let down her barriers too late to talk to her about it.

Claire made a soft sound in the back of her throat. A protest, a plea. She didn't want Mae to have gone so soon, not when she'd just—

She stood up and walked through the French doors onto the balcony. The moon was out, huge and bright.

The neighboring French doors opened and Tanner stepped outside.

He, too, had been in and around the family all day, helping where he could, just as she had. But Claire had avoided any direct contact with him.

He seemed surprised to see her there. Then he realized, "You've moved up here."

"For a couple of days, yes. Until after—"

He stepped to the railing, leaned on his elbows and looked out over the courtyard. "I'm glad Mom got here when she did. That they had a chance to mend things between them."

"I heard Jodie say she thought Mae planned everything. Even down to when she—"

"I wouldn't put it past her. Would you?"

"No."

"And the trip to cemetery hill, too."

Claire grew silent. That seemed so long ago. And yet it was just yesterday.

Tanner turned to her. "What happened to your parents, Claire?" he asked quietly. "Why were you on your own? Were they in an accident?"

"I don't want to talk about it."

He sighed and returned to his survey of the courtyard.

He was far from the ebullient person he usually was. It was because of Mae's loss, of course, but there was something more.

Several times in the day she'd noticed him standing silently and staring at nothing, as if he were in a different world. Was he thinking of his friend, as he had at the emergency room? Gloria said she'd been worried about him. And from what Claire had seen herself, losing his friend had hit him hard.

She cleared her throat. "Death is difficult to accept even when it's someone older."

"It's always difficult."

"Your friend— This must bring it all back."

"In a way."

"The outcome is the same."

He laughed without humor. "Now *I* don't want to talk about that."

Claire approached the railing, but stayed a safe distance. "I don't know anything about my parents," she said, answering his earlier question. "Who they were...where they lived. I went into care as an infant. Someone found me when I was two days old. I don't even know how I got my name. Probably someone picked it from a list."

"My God," he breathed, straightening. She could feel his eyes on her again.

She shrugged. "It happened. I don't dwell on it."

"But you don't like to talk about it."

"Would you?"

"It's nothing to be ashamed of."

"I don't like to use it as an excuse."

He was silent for a long time, then he said, "My friend's wife blames me for what happened to him."

"Why?" she asked.

"Because of the long hours Danny worked. The days he didn't get home. We built a business, had to keep it going. We both—"

"Why would she blame you and not him?"

He seemed not to hear her. "I should've told him to go home more often. Not worked such long hours myself. I didn't have any kind of life outside of work. He had a wife, a kid. Maybe he did it to keep up so I wouldn't think him a slacker."

"People make their own choices."

"Danny and I both wanted the company to succeed. But now— It wasn't worth his life. Elaine told me that she and her son probably wouldn't even miss him, because he'd never been there. Their little boy barely knew his father."

"Sometimes people say things they don't mean when they're hurting," Claire murmured.

"I'd have thought that, too, if it had only been the once—at the emergency room." He drew a sharp breath. "I had to tell her Danny was dead. But she said it at the funeral home and after the service. She was so cold. It was like she hated Danny as much as she hated me."

Claire frowned. "The two things don't go together, Tanner. If she hated him, she wouldn't blame you. She'd be relieved he was gone.''

''I loved Danny. He was like a second brother to me.''

''It's not your fault.'' She repeated the words she'd used before.

He looked at her. ''I'd give all my money back in a second if—''

''It's *not* your fault,'' she repeated firmly.

His suffering seemed to lighten as her words had impact.

''You're so easy to talk to,'' he said after a moment.

Claire moved uneasily. She was glad she'd helped him, but that was the most she felt prepared to do. ''I'm going in. It's been—''

''—a very long day,'' he finished for her.

''Yes, very long,'' she agreed. And after letting her gaze linger on him for a second, she stepped inside her temporary new bedroom and resolutely latched the door.

TANNER FORCED HIMSELF TO stay at the railing. He wanted to go to her, just to hold her. But he knew such an action wouldn't end there.

Many of the confusing things about her made sense once she'd confided her early history. The way she kept everyone at a distance—not only him—yet was at complete ease within herself. The way she didn't trust promises.

She'd changed during her short time at the ranch. She'd become more protective of Mae, more attuned to the family. As to what she felt for him—

She planned to stay at the ranch through Mae's funeral. He couldn't imagine not seeing her again after the next two days.

One concern exchanged for another.

Elaine's behavior seemed less excessive in the light of Claire's suggestion. He could handle Elaine hating him; he *couldn't* handle her hating Danny. What had torn him up inside was that he'd somehow made her hate Danny. If Claire was right...Claire *was* right! Elaine had struck out at him in pain and he had accepted the burden in similar pain.

Maybe, with the passage of time, he could try to talk to Elaine again. She and her son had no financial worries, but Tanner knew better than most that money was a cold companion. Everything he'd once dreamed about had come true, but it had brought him no joy.

Claire said people made their own choices. Danny had made his, even if he hadn't chosen to die young. Now Tanner had choices of his own to make. He had to stop drifting. Find his way.

Things were better between him and Rafe. He'd

gained his stepbrother's respect and shown him a little of what his own world was like. He felt closer to Rafe now. Closer to Rafe's family. Closer to the entire ranch clan.

But he'd yet to sort out his feelings for Claire.

And to that end, he couldn't let her leave without knowing he'd see her again.

CLAIRE STOOD OFF BY herself on the familiar hillside, partially in the shade of the trees, as family and friends crowded around the burial site. A pair of horses had drawn a wagon bearing Mae's casket—a Parker tradition, she'd learned. The ranch hands, dressed in their best gear, stood a little apart, as well, their hats in their hands, sorrow in their faces. Relations from all over the state and beyond had dropped what they were doing and come to pay tribute. A Parker who hosted a television travel show, a minor celebrity of sorts, was in attendance with his wife. Even some state politicians were there.

Darlene and Thomas had flown back from Scandinavia, Gloria had returned from Arizona with her husband.

Claire wore the only dress she'd brought with her that wasn't one of her uniforms. She hoped Mae would approve. Tanner had found a suit from somewhere, and when she'd first seen him— Well, she imagined Mae would have approved of that reaction as well.

The service ended and people returned, solemn-faced, to their cars or chose the moderate walk across open pasture to the compound. There, neighbors had set out numerous chairs in the court-yard and filled a serving table with an unbelievable quantity of food and drink. Marie and Axel hadn't needed to lift a finger.

Sadness reigned at first. Then, slowly, as people less close to the family drifted back to their busy lives, talk turned to stories about Mae. Experiences with her were relived to the point where LeRoy laughed and said, "Aunt Mae's probably up in heaven right now, watchin' all this and lovin' it!"

"You think she'd be mad because I'm here?" Lurleen asked. She was a sweet-faced woman, close to Gib in age, and she obviously thought the world of him.

"Not for a second," Gib assured her. "I told you what she said."

"And if she said it, she meant it," Jodie agreed. Her eyes were red-rimmed, but she smiled.

"I still feel like a bolt of lightning's going to come down and get me!" Lurleen murmured.

Gib tucked her close. "Well, honey, don't."

Rafe smiled wryly. "If Mae was here, she'd

probably want to plan your wedding. That woman loved weddings.''

"She did her best to take over ours," Shannon remembered. "Down to the bridesmaids' dresses. But we still managed to hang on to a few of our own ideas."

"She sure enjoyed herself, though."

"Christine and I got around that problem by elopin'," Morgan bragged.

His statement provoked derisive laughter.

Gentle teasing, poking fun…Claire could see that the family had started to recover.

An outsider might have speculated that Mae's loss would shatter the modern-day Parkers, but the outsider would be wrong. As in the past, one generation gave to the next. The line carried on.

"Would you like more iced tea?" Tanner asked. Seconds before, he'd come to stand at Claire's side.

Claire glanced down at her empty glass. She hadn't realized she'd finished it. "Uh, no. No, thanks."

"When are you planning to leave?" he asked quietly.

"I thought…later."

"Before dark?"

She nodded.

The Parkers hadn't made her leave-taking any

easier. Yesterday, the women had come to speak to her in a group. They'd thanked her for all she'd done for Mae and for them as a family, and asked her to stay longer if she'd like. That she should consider the time a vacation.

But this was already the hardest departure Claire would ever have to make. If she stayed longer—

Tanner took the glass and set it on the table. Then he pulled her with him, away from the family group.

"Tanner? What? I don't—" She faltered.

"I want to talk to you," he said. His tone brooked no objections.

He led her down the path to the ranch office, where he closed them inside the single room. Then he seated Claire in the swivel chair and rolled her back away from the desk.

Hunkering down in front of her, he asked, "Have you ever been on a cruise?" At her surprised look, he said, "Separate cabins…on different ends of the ship, for all I care. I'll pay your way. I can afford it. No commitments. No expectations. Just…let's see what happens. What do you say?"

"Tanner—"

"Something's happened between us, Claire. I want to give that something a chance—when

you're not involved with a patient and I'm not—
I don't want to not ever see you again.''

Claire shook her head. ''No, I can't do that.''

''Just for a week. A few days even. And if you
don't like the idea of a boat, stay longer at the
ranch. I know the Parkers have asked you to stay.
I heard them talking.''

Again Claire shook her head. ''No.''

''Where will you go?''

''To another patient.''

''Where?''

''I don't know.''

''Will I be able to see you?''

''That wouldn't be a good idea.''

''Claire! I *keep* my promises.''

She looked away.

''You came to care for Mae, didn't you?'' he
challenged. ''And you like the Parkers. You didn't
want to let yourself, but you do. Is that such a
terrible crime?''

He covered a hand that gripped the arm of the
chair. Claire jumped as if he'd shot her.

Mae and the Parkers had already breached one
of her defenses. She *had* to hold the other secure.

''Look,'' he said with a lopsided grin. ''I'm not
such a bad person. Some women have even gone
so far as to say I'm nice. Come on the cruise with

me. There won't be any pressure. Beautiful sunrises, beautiful sunsets.''

Claire shook her head, then shook it harder when she felt herself weaken. She didn't know what she felt for him…just that she did feel something. But she was afraid.

''I…can't.''

''I've told you I'll pay.''

''It's not that. I have some money put away. It's—'' What could she say? *I'm afraid to let myself even consider finding out what that "something" between us is.* She glanced at the closed door. ''Tanner, people saw us leave. They're going to start to wonder—''

''Let 'em wonder.''

''This is the day of Mae's funeral!''

''Mae would understand most of all. I can't let you go, Claire. Not without knowing that I'm going to see you again.''

''I can't!'' She pushed to her feet, sending the chair thumping back against the wall.

He came upright in one fluid motion and closed the distance between them. One hand rested at the side of her waist, the other tipped up her chin.

''You don't have to worry, Claire. I won't hurt you. And I won't let anyone else hurt you, either.''

She couldn't do it! She couldn't let herself entertain even the slightest glimmer of hope. Then she looked into his eyes. Always her downfall with him.

"I— I—"

He suddenly let her go. "I promise I'll be on my best behavior. We'll go as friends, nothing more." He cocked his head. "What do you think Mae would say?"

Claire knew what Mae would say. She'd told her! *Don't close yourself off so much that you don't see what's right in front of you.*

"I— She'd—" she stammered.

"She'd tell us to go," Tanner said. Then he smiled at her and Claire's resistance scattered into complete disarray.

CHAPTER SIXTEEN

TANNER PULLED A FEW strings and the next evening Claire found herself on board an amazing vessel, homeported in Miami, and about to set sail from that city for a weeklong cruise through the Caribbean.

She had to keep pinching herself to convince herself that what she was doing was real. She'd never been on a cruise ship before. Never even thought to go on one.

When she'd awakened in her cabin the first morning out, she thought she was at the ranch. Her initial instinct was to get up and check Mae.... Then she remembered.

In the beginning she'd felt a fraud among the holidaymakers. A hasty shopping trip at a Miami mall had provided clothing for the trip, but she couldn't join in with the rampant merriment.

Tanner didn't seem to mind. Each morning he called at her cabin—his was, as he'd said, a distance away. They'd walk on deck, have breakfast together, sun themselves, have lunch, gaze at the ocean, watch their fellow travelers, meet for dinner, gaze at the ocean at night, then separate at her cabin. When the ship called at a port, they made short excursions onto the islands.

He was the perfect companion, affable, attentive, but he never pressured her for anything. They were, as he'd said, acting as friends. He told her about his sisters and brother, more about his parents' life in Phoenix, and about some of his adventures growing up.

Over the days, Claire began to relax. She listened to his stories with more enjoyment, looked forward to meeting him again each morning.

She noticed the looks he seemed unaware of, coming from unattached females and some who were attached, as well. His boy-next-door good looks, his smile, his demeanor—everything about him—drew women's eyes.

As they sat side by side in deck chairs and she sketched and he read, she felt what had started out as instant attraction slowly deepen into something else. The thought frightened her, but at the same time, in this wonderful world of suspended reality, she didn't turn away from it.

She realized, as she never had before, that what she'd felt for Bryan Fitzgerald had little to do with actual male-female attraction. That's why he'd

been so shocked when he'd come to recognize
what she'd concocted in her mind. He hadn't
meant to hurt her.

She'd wanted a family so badly. She'd wanted
to belong. She'd thought to slip in and make things
right for the Fitzgeralds as she made things right
for herself. Naively.

Was she being naive about Tanner, as well?
Running away from him when she should be running toward him?

The final night of the cruise arrived. The passengers' luggage had to be in the hall by midnight,
ready to be collected. Claire had little to pack. Her
wardrobe trunk had come with her. She secured it
and waited for the steward to help her get it outside. Tanner, she knew, was doing the same thing
in his cabin.

She'd left out the pretty seashell Tanner had
found on an island beach and casually handed to
her as they'd strolled along the sand. She'd yet to
add it to her collection of keepsakes, unsure if she
should.

Someone tapped on her door. The steward? It
was Tanner.

"Need help with that?" he offered.

"The steward's coming soon," she said.

Before the last word had fully left her lips, the
uniformed man showed up with a dolly cart,

slipped it into place under the trunk, rolled it outside, set it against the wall and cheerfully wished them a nice evening. Then he was off to his next appointment.

"Amazing people," Tanner murmured as he watched the steward depart. "They work all hours of the day and night."

"And manage to be friendly, too," Claire added in agreement.

From the doorway, Tanner glanced around her cabin. "Are you going to miss this place?"

"Are you? Will you miss yours?"

"I've had a good time. So, yes, probably."

His eyes alighted on the shell on her dressing table. Next to her small carryall with her overnight things.

"The week's gone by fast," he said.

"Yes," she answered quietly.

She could feel the tension that had been mounting in him all day. The same tension that had grown inside her. Tomorrow morning they would be back in Miami. By tomorrow afternoon— Neither had spoken of tomorrow afternoon.

"How about one last stroll on deck?" he proposed.

"I'd like that," she said.

THE WANING MOON LOOKED beautiful against the dark surface of the water. The breeze was warm, tropical. Music and laughter floated up from the parties taking place within the ship. A scattering of other passengers also roamed the deck—some singly, some as couples, some in groups.

Tanner walked alongside Claire with his hands in his pockets. If he didn't, he wouldn't be able to stop himself from touching her. He'd wanted to do more than touch her all week, but he'd held himself firmly in check. He'd made a promise that he wasn't going to break. He had to show her that she could trust him.

As the days and hours ticked away, though, he began to wonder what else he could do. Were they any further along in defining their relationship than they had been when they'd first set foot on the ship? He'd felt her relax several days into the voyage. And since, she'd been more freely accommodating. But he didn't have a true sense of a connection with her. Was it because he'd been holding back?

Tomorrow morning she could walk out of his life. If he didn't say something now—

He guided her to the railing. She caught hold of it; he rested his elbows on the cool metal. His heart pounded beneath his calm exterior. What he was about to say and do could affect the rest of his life. He didn't care that much about what he did to occupy his time anymore. He'd find something. It was *her* he wanted. Claire.

"Have, uh, have you enjoyed the cruise?" he asked, glancing at her.

"Surprisingly, yes."

"You didn't expect to?"

"I thought—" She stopped.

He made himself smile. "What? That I'd gone insane?"

She copied his smile. "Well, maybe a little."

"Do you think that now?"

She shook her head.

He shifted position and trailed a finger over the back of her hand. Lightly, like a butterfly's kiss. "I'm glad you came."

He hadn't meant for that to come out quite so huskily, quite so revealing.

"I'm glad I did, too," she said.

Had she trembled?

He turned to look at her. "Are you cool?" he asked. The moonlight did wonderful things to her skin, darkened the shadow of her eyelashes, high-lighted the pale threads in her short hair.

"A little."

Tanner wasn't the least bit cool. "Would you like my jacket?"

She shook her head negatively.

He braced himself. "Claire—" he started, then

had to start again. He decided to be straightforward. "I want you to come with me to Phoenix. Or I'll go with you wherever you go. I don't— I can't be away from you. I can't let you walk out of my life tomorrow and pretend I don't care. I *do* care. I care more now than—"

She looked up at him and his breath caught. She was the most beautiful woman he'd ever seen. Not a period painting, not a watercolor. A living woman only a step away that he wanted to kiss more than he wanted life itself.

"I've never been to Phoenix," she said softly.

For a second he wasn't sure if he'd heard her correctly. He looked at her, wondering if he'd been mistaken.

"I think I'd like to go there," she added.

A burning warmth such as Tanner had never experienced before burst through his body. A happiness he'd never known. He'd been afraid that she'd still want to hold him off. That this week had done nothing to further his cause.

"Claire!" he exclaimed brokenly, and pulled her against him. Then he quickly let her go. He'd promised!

She lifted her face and smiled at him. A smile he'd never received from her before. Then she stepped shyly back into his arms.

Tanner kissed her and held her and kissed her again.

Finally, becoming aware of the scattered passengers around them, he gained control.

"Tell me this is real," he demanded, holding her slightly away from him.

"I can't!" she answered, laughter in her voice.

Had he heard her laugh before? Really laugh?

"Tell me!" he demanded. He had to hear her say it.

"I— Tanner— I'm not very good at this. You— you'll have to give me more time before I can— What I do know is that I don't want to leave you tomorrow. You're— I—" She seemed unable to go on.

"That's enough," he assured her quickly, and pulled her back against him. "We'll go from there."

He loved her. It was as simple and as complex as that.

And he would wait until she let herself love him.

EPILOGUE

THE LITTLE BLUE SPORTS CAR ate up the miles of sunbaked terrain as Claire and Tanner returned to the Parker Ranch.

Tanner glanced at her and squeezed her hand. "Are you still nervous about going back?" he asked.

"A little," she admitted.

The closer they came to the ranch, the more of Claire's old reticence returned. She wasn't sure how she would be received. She'd come to the ranch the first time to do a job. Now she was with Tanner.

"Rafe extended the invitation himself," Tanner said. "They *want* to see us."

"I know, but everything is so different."

"Yes." Tanner grinned and carried her hand to his lips. He kissed her finger on either side of the engagement ring.

They turned onto the narrow road that led past ranch headquarters, then eventually, into the far arm of the U-shaped drive.

Claire's stomach tightened as they rolled past the houses and the courtyard to stop in front of the main house. The yellow Lab, asleep on the front porch, started to his feet and barked.

"Junior…hey, boy, it's us!" Tanner called as he stepped out onto the gravel drive.

The dog instantly switched from guard duty to welcoming committee. With his ears laid back and his tail wagging furiously, he bounded off the porch to meet them.

Doors opened all over the compound, followed by hailed greetings.

As Claire stepped out of the car, Rafe and Shannon, Harriet and LeRoy and Gib all converged on the spot.

Shannon and Harriet didn't hesitate. They took turns hugging Claire as if she was a longtime friend.

Tanner winked at Claire and rested a protective arm around her shoulders as they all moved into the house.

Marie hurried out of the kitchen and more greetings were exchanged. Claire felt overwhelmed by the outpouring of good will.

The living room looked far different from the last time Claire had seen it six months ago. More in keeping with a growing family. Comfortable couches and chairs, different curtains. Toys scattered about on the floor. Gib's painting of ranch headquarters still held place of honor over the mantel, though, and his painting of Rafe hung proudly on another wall.

"Mae said in her letter to toss everything out and start over," Shannon explained, "but we couldn't do that. We put some things in storage and spread the rest around."

"It took a month before we could convince 'em they should move into the place," Gib said. "They were almost as stubborn as Marie and Axel."

"They picked out the spot for their house last week," Shannon said. "Just a little way back from the barn. Marie's thrilled, but she won't admit it."

"Wes has moved into Rafe and Shannon's old place," LeRoy added. "He was ready to be on his own."

Harriet grinned. "And Gwen moved into his old room, so she and Anna each have rooms to themselves now, too."

"Aunt Mae knew what she was doin'," Rafe said quietly.

Little Nikki toddled over to her mother and Shannon lifted her onto her lap.

Rafe looked at his stepbrother. "So, you two are plannin' to get hitched, we hear."

"Sure are." Tanner grinned, his arm tightening around Claire.

"Does that mean you'll be goin' back to bein' one a' them there *computer moguls?*" LeRoy teased.

"Nope. I'm looking around, but not for something like that. If Claire and I have kids, we want them to know who their daddy is."

"What about you, Claire?" Shannon asked. "Will you continue nursing?"

Claire shrugged. "Probably. For a while. I like doing it."

"You should," Rafe declared, surprising her with his approval. "You're good at it."

Marie returned with coffee and cake and fresh fruit.

As their visit extended, Tanner went off with the men—Rafe wanted to show him how well the computer system for the ranch records functioned—and Claire settled in with the women. They were curious about her and Tanner and wanted to hear everything she'd tell them about the past six months.

"I always thought there was somethin' goin' on there," Harriet claimed.

"You didn't." Shannon laughed.

"I'm surprised Aunt Mae didn't put a hand in herself." Harriet looked momentarily pensive.

"That last week…she wasn't at the top of her form," Shannon murmured. Then to Claire, she added, "You should have met her a few years back. She had her hand in everything. No one was safe. She brought me to the ranch to marry Rafe, you know. Only I didn't know it! Good thing…I would never have come."

"And I have my suspicions she got LeRoy and me together, without us knowin' it, either."

Claire kept her own counsel.

A SHORT TIME LATER CLAIRE and Tanner made their way up cemetery hill to visit Mae's grave. There was a timelessness about the place. A timelessness about the view.

They walked to Mae's grave and stood looking at it a long time.

"We'd never have met if she hadn't brought you here," Tanner said.

"And Rafe brought you here," she returned softly.

She reached into her pocket and brought out the shell Tanner had given her during the cruise. She set it into the slight mound of rocky soil near the marker.

"I want her to have it," Claire said.

Tanner nodded silently.

Mae Parker might think she had a lot to answer for to her Parker relatives in heaven. But Claire would always know that the woman had given more to her than she could ever pay back.

She'd learned to trust and learned to love, and in the end, gained two families—the Reids of Arizona and the Parkers of West Texas.

And the family she and Tanner would one day create.

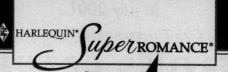

HARLEQUIN *Super* ROMANCE®

RETURN TO
EAST
TEXAS

**After twenty years, they all come back—
Jed and Emmy and Will—to find the solution to
a long-buried mystery: *Why did their foster
mother, Frannie Granger, die? Who killed her?*
After twenty years, they're looking
for answers...and for love.**

Join them in the town of Uncertain, Texas!

Enjoy this captivating trilogy

The Millionaire Horseman by **K.N. Casper,**
on sale in April 2001

Who Is Emerald Monday? by **Roz Denny Fox,**
on sale in May 2001

A Man of His Word by **Eve Gaddy,**
on sale in June 2001

Available wherever Harlequin books are sold.

HARLEQUIN®
Makes any time special ®

Visit us at www.eHarlequin.com

HSRRET

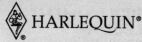

INDULGE IN A QUIET MOMENT
WITH HARLEQUIN

Get a FREE
Quiet Moments Bath Spa

**with just two proofs of purchase from
any of our four special collector's editions in May.**

**Harlequin® is sure to make your time special this Mother's Day
with four special collector's editions featuring a short story
PLUS a complete novel packaged together in one volume!**

Collection #1 Intrigue abounds in a collection featuring *New York Times*
bestselling author Barbara Delinsky and Kelsey Roberts.

Collection #2 Relationships? Weddings? Children? = *New York Times*
bestselling author Debbie Macomber and Tara Taylor Quinn
at their best!

Collection #3 Escape to the past with *New York Times* bestselling author
Heather Graham and Gayle Wilson.

Collection #4 Go West! With *New York Times* bestselling author
Joan Johnston and Vicki Lewis Thompson!

Plus Special Consumer Campaign!
Each of these four collector's editions will feature a
"FREE QUIET MOMENTS BATH SPA" offer.
See inside book in May for details.

Only from
◆ HARLEQUIN®
Makes any time special ®

Don't miss out! Look for this exciting promotion on sale in May 2001,
at your favorite retail outlet.

Visit us at www.eHarlequin.com   PHNCP01

Harlequin truly does make any time special. . . . This year we are celebrating weddings in style!

A Walk Down the Aisle
WEDDING CELEBRATION

To help us celebrate, we want you to tell us how wearing the Harlequin wedding gown will make your wedding day special. As the grand prize, Harlequin will offer one lucky bride the chance to **"Walk Down the Aisle"** in the Harlequin wedding gown!

There's more...

For her honeymoon, she and her groom will spend five nights at the **Hyatt Regency Maui.** As part of this five-night honeymoon at the hotel renowned for its romantic attractions, the couple will enjoy a candlelit dinner for two in Swan Court, a sunset sail on the hotel's catamaran, and duet spa treatments.

Maui • Molokai • Lanai

To enter, please write, in, 250 words or less, how wearing the Harlequin wedding gown will make your wedding day special. The entry will be judged based on its emotionally compelling nature, its originality and creativity, and its sincerity. This contest is open to Canadian and U.S. residents only and to those who are 18 years of age and older. There is no purchase necessary to enter. Void where prohibited. See further contest rules attached. Please send your entry to:

Walk Down the Aisle Contest

In Canada	In U.S.A.
P.O. Box 637	P.O. Box 9076
Fort Erie, Ontario	3010 Walden Ave.
L2A 5X3	Buffalo, NY 14269-9076

You can also enter by visiting www.eHarlequin.com
Win the Harlequin wedding gown and the vacation of a lifetime!
The deadline for entries is October 1, 2001.

HARLEQUIN®
Makes any time special ®

PHWDACONT1

HARLEQUIN WALK DOWN THE AISLE TO MAUI CONTEST 1197
OFFICIAL RULES
NO PURCHASE NECESSARY TO ENTER

1. To enter, follow directions published in the offer to which you are responding. Contest begins April 2, 2001, and ends on October 1, 2001. Method of entry may vary. Mailed entries must be postmarked by October 1, 2001, and received by October 8, 2001.

2. Contest entry may be, at times, presented via the Internet, but will be restricted solely to residents of certain geographic areas that are disclosed on the Web site. To enter via the Internet, if permissible, access the Harlequin Web site (www.eHarlequin.com) and follow the directions displayed online. Online entries must be received by 11:59 p.m. E.S.T. on October 1, 2001.

   In lieu of submitting an entry online, enter by mail by hand-printing (or typing) on an 8½" x 11" plain piece of paper, your name, address (including zip code), Contest number/name and in 250 words or fewer, why winning a Harlequin wedding dress would make your wedding day special. Mail via first-class mail to: Harlequin Walk Down the Aisle Contest 1197, (in the U.S.) P.O. Box 9076, 3010 Walden Avenue, Buffalo, NY 14269-9076, (in Canada) P.O. Box 637, Fort Erie, Ontario L2A 5X3, Canada. Limit one entry per person, household address and e-mail address. Online and/or mailed entries received from persons residing in geographic areas in which Internet entry is not permissible will be disqualified.

3. Contests will be judged by a panel of members of the Harlequin editorial, marketing and public relations staff based on the following criteria:

   * Originality and Creativity—50%
   * Emotionally Compelling—25%
   * Sincerity—25%

   In the event of a tie, duplicate prizes will be awarded. Decisions of the judges are final.

4. All entries become the property of Torstar Corp. and will not be returned. No responsibility is assumed for lost, late, illegible, incomplete, inaccurate, nondelivered or misdirected mail or misdirected e-mail, for technical, hardware or software failures of any kind, lost or unavailable network connections, or failed, incomplete, garbled or delayed computer transmission or any human error which may occur in the receipt or processing of the entries in this Contest.

5. Contest open only to residents of the U.S. (except Puerto Rico) and Canada, who are 18 years of age or older, and is void wherever prohibited by law; all applicable laws and regulations apply. Any litigation within the Province of Quebec respecting the conduct or organization of a publicity contest may be submitted to the Régie des alcools, des courses et des jeux for a ruling. Any litigation respecting the awarding of a prize may be submitted to the Régie des alcools, des courses et des jeux only for the purpose of helping the parties reach a settlement. Employees and immediate family members of Torstar Corp. and D. L. Blair, Inc., their affiliates, subsidiaries and all other agencies, entities and persons connected with the use, marketing or conduct of this Contest are not eligible to enter. Taxes on prizes are the sole responsibility of winners. Acceptance of any prize offered constitutes permission to use winner's name, photograph or other likeness for the purposes of advertising, trade and promotion on behalf of Torstar Corp., its affiliates and subsidiaries without further compensation to the winner, unless prohibited by law.

6. Winners will be determined no later than November 15, 2001, and will be notified by mail. Winners will be required to sign and return an Affidavit of Eligibility form within 15 days after winner notification. Noncompliance within that time period may result in disqualification and an alternative winner may be selected. Winners of trip must execute a Release of Liability prior to ticketing and must possess required travel documents (e.g. passport, photo ID) where applicable. Trip must be completed by November 2002. No substitution of prize permitted by winner. Torstar Corp. and D. L. Blair, Inc., their parents, affiliates, and subsidiaries are not responsible for errors in printing or electronic presentation of Contest, entries and/or game pieces. In the event of printing or other errors which may result in unintended prize values or duplication of prizes, all affected game pieces or entries shall be null and void. If for any reason the Internet portion of the Contest is not capable of running as planned, including infection by computer virus, bugs, tampering, unauthorized intervention, fraud, technical failures, or any other causes beyond the control of Torstar Corp. which corrupt or affect the administration, secrecy, fairness, integrity or proper conduct of the Contest, Torstar Corp. reserves the right, at its sole discretion, to disqualify any individual who tampers with the entry process and to cancel, terminate, modify or suspend the Contest or the Internet portion thereof. In the event of a dispute regarding an online entry, the entry will be deemed submitted by the authorized holder of the e-mail account submitted at the time of entry. Authorized account holder is defined as the natural person who is assigned to an e-mail address by an Internet access provider, online service provider or other organization that is responsible for arranging e-mail address for the domain associated with the submitted e-mail address. **Purchase or acceptance of a product offer does not improve your chances of winning.**

7. Prizes: (1) Grand Prize—A Harlequin wedding dress (approximate retail value: $3,500) and a 5-night/6-day honeymoon trip to Maui, HI, including round-trip air transportation provided by Maui Visitors Bureau from Los Angeles International Airport (winner is responsible for transportation to and from Los Angeles International Airport) and a Harlequin Romance Package, including hotel accomodations (double occupancy) at the Hyatt Regency Maui Resort and Spa, dinner for 2 two at Swan Court, a sunset sail on Kiele V and a spa treatment for the winner (approximate retail value: $4,000); (5) Five runner-up prizes of a $1000 gift certificate to selected retail outlets to be determined by Sponsor (retail value $1000 ea.). Prizes consist of only those items listed as part of the prize. Limit one prize per person. All prizes are valued in U.S. currency.

8. For a list of winners (available after December 17, 2001) send a self-addressed, stamped envelope to: Harlequin Walk Down Aisle Contest 1197 Winners, P.O. Box 4200 Blair, NE 68009-4200 or you may access the www.eHarlequin.com Web site through January 15, 2002.

Contest sponsored by Torstar Corp., P.O. Box 9042, Buffalo, NY 14269-9042, U.S.A.

PHWDACONT2

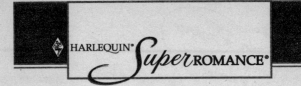